# THE PARROT MATCHMAKER

# THE PARROT MATCHMAKER

## AN AFRICAN LOVERS TALE

### Felix Adeoti Oguntoye

ASALAKO
PRESS

Book:    ISBN-13:   978-0-9891630-2-6
e-Book:  ISBN:        978-0-9891630-3-3

Printed in the United States of America
10  9  8  7  6  5  4  3  2  1

Published by Asalako Press
http://www. asalakopress.com

## ONE

emi and his family lived in a little village in the forest. His father was the poorest of peasants, and his mother sold firewood. They lived in abject poverty, and Remi had to help his mother with collecting the firewood so that everyone would have something to eat.

Although some forests were better than others, firewood was generally hard to find. They spent so much time and energy in locating, gathering, cutting, and seasoning the wood. With ax and machete, Remi and his mother cut down whole trees, trimmed and cut the branches, and stacked the wood to dry. They braided palm fronds together and covered the wood so that passersby would know the wood belonged to someone; otherwise, they would lose the wood and waste a day's work.

Sometimes they were lucky enough to find wood that was already dry—branches that had blown off trees or whole trees that had fallen. These could be cut and taken home for immediate sale. Because this work brought a faster return for their labor, Remi and his mother would bind these dry branches and trees with vines and make as many trips home as needed.

Remi and his mother carried firewood to the market on market day, and they also sold it in nearby villages. They had regular customers, but they also kept track of who was going to have a feast on a special occasion, as these people would need extra wood to cook for their guests.

And they also sold leaves to the merchants who sold prepared food. The leaves served as plates, and these merchants always needed a fresh supply.

Remi also helped his father on their little farm, but the land was so barren that they received very little produce for their labor, and there was nothing left over to sell. They could not afford to hire anyone to help, so Remi and his sister Ranti did most of the work. In fact, their whole lives were taken up with painstaking work, for they had only the clothes on their backs and could not afford to go to parties or enjoy other frivolities like most of the other teenagers in their village.

Ranti, however, did have a chance to meet and befriend some of the other girls in nearby villages. It was through her that Remi found out about Aderonke.

Aderonke was simply astounding. She was the most beautiful girl for miles around, but unlike many beautiful girls, she was not stuck up about her looks. She was good-natured and friendly, quiet and gentle, charming and intelligent. In short, Aderonke was a paragon.

One day Remi happened to accompany his sister to the village where Aderonke lived, and he got to meet Aderonke very briefly. Afterward, he talked to his sister about her.

"Aderonke is incredibly beautiful!" he exclaimed as soon as they were out of earshot. "Why didn't you tell me how absolutely beautiful she is?"

Ranti laughed and said, "Of course, she's beautiful. I told you so, but you never paid any attention."

"Well, she is a model of perfection," Remi marveled. "What a wife she will make! Do you think there is anything I can do to win her love?"

"Oh, Remi! Do you have any idea how many young men want to marry her? Aderonke has been the talk of villages many miles from here, and every eligible bachelor asks the same question. She has been getting all kinds of presents from hopeful suitors, but she can marry only one of them."

"But who does not want something truly beautiful?" Remi asked earnestly. "If she were only pretty, it would mean little, but she is beautiful in every respect. How many women are both gorgeous and good-natured? How many are not only intelligent but friendly and charming, too? Isn't there some way you can influence her? After all, she has to marry someone. Who knows which man she will choose?"

"Well," his sister said, "I suppose we can try. But you know how poor we are. If I were looking for a husband, I should certainly look for one who had some property."

Remi shook his head sadly. He had little to say the rest of the way home because he was thinking hard.

*I am old enough to get a wife,* he thought, *but not wealthy enough to have one. This is such a hard world—the one who has corn does not have the teeth to chew it! I wish I had all kinds of money.... I'd overwhelm Aderonke with presents. I'd give her better presents than anyone else, and then she would want to marry me. Life has been unkind to my parents, and now it is unkind to me. Why don't I have any money? Providence, please be merciful to me! Let this poverty come to an end! Too much money may be a headache, but right now I would rather have the headache! Please, Providence, bless me with prosperity!*

That night Remi could hardly eat. All he could do was think about Aderonke. He did not talk to Ranti

about it because she was helping their mother prepare supper. After supper, he went straight to bed.

That night Remi had a dream.

In his dream, Remi decided he would gain access
to Aderonke's house. Even though he could think
of no really good excuse for going there, he went
anyway. When he approached her house, a vicious
black dog ran out and frightened him away, but
Remi did not go far.

Aderonke came out of the house on an errand.
She had to buy some palm oil for her parents. Remi
was able to see her clearly, and just as it had when
Remi first saw her in real life, his heart turned over
in his chest.

"Hello, Aderonke!" he cried joyfully.

Aderonke did not answer. Instead, she stared at
him coldly and then went on her way.

Poor Remi! He was disappointed but not
discouraged. Perhaps Aderonke was tired of young
men constantly trying to win her favor. Remi followed
her along the road, but he did not try to catch up to
her or talk to her.

As they walked along, Aderonke's path crossed
that of one of her suitors. This young man came up
to Aderonke and put his arm around her shoulder.
Together they went to the palm-oil seller, and when

they got there, the young man went into the shop with Aderonke.

Remi waited outside impatiently. It did not make him very happy to lose sight of Aderonke, but he was even less pleased when she emerged from the shop still talking and laughing with her suitor.

Of course, Aderonke and her suitor ignored Remi, and of course, Remi followed them.

"Aderonke," the suitor began, "What in the world do you have in common with that poor peasant who is following you around? He has no means to support you or even to give you a present!"

Unfortunately, the suitor did not stop at this. He began jeering at Remi and insulting him. The result was a fight. Although Remi was poor, he was an exceptionally good fighter. Every time Aderonke's loudmouth suitor came at him, Remi knocked him down.

The fight attracted some onlookers, and when they saw how Remi kept knocking down Aderonke's suitor, they began to cheer for Remi and make fun of the suitor. No one had expected such a poor peasant to prove himself a skilled fighter. The suitor was eventually helped to his home, limping in disgrace.

Aderonke started home again, but a sudden shower brought torrents of rain. She took shelter on the veranda of a building along the road, and Remi took shelter there, too. He gathered all his courage and spoke to her.

"You should not stay here long, Aderonke. It is getting dark, and it would not be safe to be out in such a rain after dark," he said sincerely. "You might slip in the mud and hurt yourself or lose your way home. And your parents will be worried. If you would like, I will run to my house—it's not very far away—and bring you a calabash to keep the rain from drenching you."

Aderonke did not seem too pleased to have Remi speak to her again, but she appeared to appreciate his good sense.

Remi ran to his house and got the big calabash that his mother often used for carrying sizable loads of leaves to market.

"Remi! What are you doing?" his mother cried. "I need the calabash early in the morning. Where are you taking it?"

"I will explain later!" Remi shouted as he raced out the door and into the rainstorm. Remi handed Aderonke the calabash when he reached her again. Aderonke seemed surprised that Remi had come back at all, but she turned the calabash upside down over her head and stepped out into the driving rain.

The rain was coming down so hard that Aderonke could not see Remi once again following her. She slipped several times, and once a gust of windblown rain nearly knocked her over. But soon Aderonke reached her parents' home.

At the same time, Aderonke's mother stepped out the door. She wore a large rain hat and carried a strong staff in her hand.

"Aderonke!" she cried. "Where in the world have you been? You are so late coming home, and I have just now come out into the rain to find you! Why are you such a bad girl?"

Remi could see that Aderonke's mother was extremely angry because she had been terribly worried about her daughter. With the rain pouring about his ears, he stepped forward and spoke to her.

"The storm was very fierce," he hollered, "and Aderonke could not even see where she was going because of the rain in her eyes! She had to take shelter. I brought her the calabash to keep the water out of her eyes, and I followed her home to make sure she arrived safely. I assure you that she has come as quickly as possible, and I hope you will not be angry with her."

Aderonke's mother quit fussing at Aderonke and smiled at Remi. "Thank you, young man," she said. "I am very grateful that you have seen Aderonke safely home. Tell me. What is your name, and who are your parents? They have a thoughtful son."

"My name is Remi. My father is Toye, and my mother is Tohun," Remi answered.

"Ah!" Aderonke's mother exclaimed. "I should have known!"

Both Aderonke and Remi were bewildered.

Aderonke's mother explained, "Before either of you were born, back when I was a girl, there was a famine. We had no money then—you see, Aderonke, we have not always been lucky—and my mother would go to Remi's grandmother to buy corn. That was the only food we had at the time. My mother would arrange to buy on credit, and she would promise to pay the next market day. But we were so poor that my mother never got enough money on the promised date." Aderonke's mother paused and then smiled sweetly before continuing. "Remi, she would still go back to your grandmother to buy more on credit, and your grandmother never once turned her down. You are the grandson of a kind and generous person. No wonder you are so nice—it runs in the family! May the soul of your grandmother rest in peace, Remi."

Remi nodded and then took the calabash. Aderonke's mother admonished him to be careful and to get home quickly because it was getting darker by the minute. She asked Remi to greet his mother for her, but Aderonke never said one word of thanks or farewell. As Remi turned toward home, he woke up.

It had seemed so real! One moment, Remi's happiness evaporated as he realized the encounter was only imaginary.

But why should he have dreamed such a vivid dream? Remi pondered for a long time, and the more he thought about it, the more intense his feelings became for Aderonke. All day long, he contemplated the details of his strange and wonderful dream.

He could not even talk to his sister about it because he did not see her that day. And the next day, he had to go to the farm. By the time he returned, Ranti had left again to attend a wedding in another village. All this time, Remi pondered his dream.

Was it true that Aderonke's family had once been poor? Had his own grandmother actually helped Aderonke's grandmother? Would Aderonke's mother welcome his affection for Aderonke? And even if she did, what good would that do if Aderonke was not in the least interested in him? After all, he was certainly poor. How could he afford any wife, let alone such a lovely wife as Aderonke from such a wealthy family?

That night Remi dreamed again.

In this dream, just as before, Remi decided to go to Aderonke's house. He could think of no good excuse for doing so, but he went anyway. The big black dog once again ran out and frightened him away as soon as he came close to the house. But again, Remi did not go far.

Aderonke again came out of the house to go to the market. Remi was overjoyed to see her, and he called her name.

"Hello, Aderonke!"

Remi assumed she would be glad to see him after he had rescued her from the terrible storm and from being scolded by her mother. But again, Aderonke did not answer.

Remi was not the sort of young man who took no for an answer. Aderonke might be aloof, but he would be persistent. And who knew what danger he might rescue her from today? So Remi again followed Aderonke along the path to town.

And who, of all people, should cross their path? The same young man who had so insulted Remi previously! He acted quite familiar with Aderonke, who did not seem to mind his attentions in the least. Laughing and talking, the two young people went to the market, while Remi followed along, jealous and unhappy.

He followed them all through the market, and they completely ignored him the entire time. If Remi had been awake instead of dreaming, he would have thought he was making a terrible fool of himself by following this girl and her suitor around.

Finally, the suitor said to Aderonke, "Look, Aderonke, that peasant is following you around again! You should let him follow you home and be eaten by your dog—every dog likes to gnaw on a bag of bones once in a while! He's no good for anything else, you know. He doesn't have any money."

Things went from bad to worse. The suitor became even more abusive than last time, and Remi again attacked him in anger. Remi might have been poor, but he was agile and smart and an excellent fighter. Aderonke's suitor was better with his mouth than with his fists, so Remi had no trouble at all beating him thoroughly into the ground.

Once again, the fight attracted a crowd, and once again, the crowd cheered for the clear winner: Remi. When the suitor gave up, a couple men in the crowd carried him home.

Aderonke started home, but it was not raining this time. Nevertheless, the ground was rather slippery, and there were several nasty mudholes along the path. Again, Remi followed Aderonke along the path.

Suddenly, Aderonke slipped on some wet leaves and slid right into a giant puddle. Remi would certainly have laughed to see such a strong-willed girl go sprawling into the mud, except that this strong-willed girl was his beloved Aderonke. Genuinely concerned, he rushed up to help her.

"Aderonke!" he cried. "Are you all right? Let me help you up!"

Aderonke glared at him. "You again!" she said, gritting her teeth. "I am perfectly all right, thank you! Oh!" Aderonke turned pale. "I—I think I have sprained my ankle!"

"Give me your hand," Remi said, "and I will see about your ankle."

Aderonke gave him her hand, and Remi tenderly helped her up. She was all muddy, and she got Remi muddy, but he did not care. She leaned against a tree, and Remi checked her ankle. Sure enough, it was badly sprained and already swelling unpleasantly.

"I will have to help you home," Remi said.

And that is what he did. He walked to Aderonke's house with his arm around her waist and her arm over his shoulder. All the same, Aderonke was not particularly friendly.

Aderonke's mother was outside when they arrived, and she cried, "Aderonke! What has happened to you?"

"She slipped and fell in the mud," Remi explained. "I think she has sprained her ankle. You can see that it is terribly swollen."

"Is this so, Aderonke?" her mother asked.

"Yes, Mother," Aderonke said, "I cannot walk by myself."

"You should be more careful," her mother chided. She looked at Remi, and he thought her look seemed somewhat suspicious.

*Could she think that I pushed Aderonke and caused her injury?* he wondered.

"Remi," she said, "I thank you once again for helping my daughter. Please carry my greetings to your mother."

Remi bade them farewell and hurried home. He gathered some fruit he had brought back from the farm—pawpaws, bananas, and other good things that Aderonke might like—and carefully arranged it in a basket. He carried these items back to Aderonke's house and presented the basket to her mother.

"I have brought these fruits for Aderonke," he said. "I am sure she will not be able to get about very well for the next few days, and they might make her feel better."

Aderonke's mother tried to refuse the gift, saying that Remi had already done much more than they could have asked, but Remi was persistent. She eventually agreed to take the fruit to Aderonke, and Remi woke up as he stepped onto the path to go home.

Of course, Remi was sad that the dream had been only a dream, but again it set him to thinking. Was there some way he could actually get to speak to Aderonke, to help her, to send her a gift?

He had to go to the farm again the next day, and the entire time he worked, he could think of nothing but Aderonke. That evening when he returned home, he was glad to see that Ranti had also returned from the wedding celebration. While they were eating dinner, he recounted both of his dreams to his sister and his mother.

"What do you think?" he asked after he had finished telling them about the dreams.

"Well," his mother said slowly, "I know there was a famine when I was very young. I don't remember anything about it, though. I do know my mother used to sell on credit to people who had no money. She used to say that if they starved, they could not pay at all, but if they were fed, they would eventually pay. That turned out not to be entirely true. One of the reasons we are so poor today is that many of those people never paid her back, even when they were no longer poor. My mother was a very generous person, but I think she was perhaps a little too generous at times. I don't know about

Aderonke's grandmother, though. It may be true if what the dream says is true, but Aderonke's family has been wealthy as long as I can remember."

"I wonder if Aderonke's family paid our grandmother," Ranti interjected thoughtfully.

"Oh, I am certain of it!" Remi protested. "They are well thought of! They could not be dishonest!"

"You are just in love with Aderonke!" she replied with a laugh. "You think the whole family is perfect!"

"Now, now," their mother intervened, "you must not tease Remi. He has a generous heart, and it is good that he thinks well of his neighbors. But it is certainly hard to be poor. I never go anywhere because I have no suitable clothing to wear for visiting or for attending festivals. I have no money to buy gifts. You yourself could not have gone to the wedding had not your dear friend given you a new dress to wear. And as for Remi, it will be hard on him when he seeks a wife. It is not easy to bear insults, and not all friends are as generous as yours, dear. A poor person who tries to befriend a wealthy one is usually just punishing himself."

"That is true," Aderonke's sister agreed. "I am fortunate to have a good friend who has a little money and who is willing to share with me. Remi has no such friend."

"And it is certain he will not find such a friend in Aderonke's family," their mother said. "They have been to the city, you know, and they have made a great deal of money. The only reason they are back here in the village is that Aderonke's father is the only son and must take care of the family property. Aderonke's parents regard themselves as quite superior to everyone else in the village. They keep very much to themselves and do not wish to be friends with anyone around here. I suppose the village people are too poor for them. Heaven knows we are!"

Remi thought his mother looked sad, and he was right. She was secretly wondering why Aderonke's family had never extended the hand of friendship to her own family when they were in such great need if Aderonke's mother still remembered Remi's grandmother's unfailing generosity. She shook her head. *Well,* she thought, *if they are proud, so am I. I have worked all my life and do not want to depend on anyone.*

After their mother left the room, Remi and Ranti continued to discuss the problem of Aderonke.

"Aderonke is really a rather nice girl," his sister said. "She has been the center of a great deal of attention, though. Her parents think there is no young lady in the world as wonderful as Aderonke. As you know, she has scores of suitors. Men from villages all around here—and I think some from the city, too—want to marry her. They visit her and tell her how wonderful she is and bring her presents.

She thinks she is supposed to be the center of everything. And she's rather placid, too. If someone gives her something, she accepts it. As a result, she has a considerable number of suitors and a considerable number of presents. But, you know, some of those suitors are going to start fighting among themselves sooner or later. One of them might even try to force her to marry him. I don't think Aderonke realizes how much trouble her indecision could lead to."

"I understand what you're saying," Remi said, "but who in the world does not want something beautiful? I can see why all the suitors are gathered around, and I can see why Aderonke thinks everything they give her is lovely. But I agree with you—someone is going to cause trouble one of these days."

"She is also naive," Ranti explained. "Her parents have always given her gifts and paid a great deal of attention to her, and now she accepts the same from all these men. What she fails to realize is that these gifts are costing the men money, and they are looking for a wife."

"I've got to do something about it," Remi resolved.

"Do something? Why, whatever in the world can you do about it?" she asked. "You may as well try to stop the river as to stop these men from paying attention to Aderonke! She is being rather silly, but the only thing that will settle matters is for her father to marry her off to one of the suitors. And even then, there's likely to be a fight!"

"I'll tell you what I can do about it," Remi said confidently. "I can woo her myself!"

"Remi! You cannot be serious! You have no money, and Aderonke's family is rich!" Ranti blurted out.

Undeterred, Remi said, "I certainly am serious. Nobody can get something for nothing. Whoever tries the hardest will win her."

"I would think your dream would teach you better," his sister reasoned. "In your dream, it did not matter that you helped Aderonke in the storm and when she sprained her ankle. It did not matter even that you beat her obnoxious suitor. It did not matter that her family should be indebted to ours either. And a gift of fruit would certainly look puny next to the gifts from all her rich suitors!"

"You said you would help me," Remi pleaded.

"I know, and I will try to help you if I can. But what in the world can I do?"

"She is your friend," Remi answered. "You can talk to her anytime you like. You can get to her, and I can't. If you were to spend more time with her, you might be able to determine if there were some way I could woo her. Maybe you could learn something useful. Perhaps you could find a way for me to get a chance to talk to Aderonke for more than just a moment."

"Of course, I will do that, Remi," Ranti promised. "And I have some money I have been putting aside from selling the brooms and mats. That might provide a nice little present to catch her attention for you. I will see if she can come out for a walk this evening so that you can have a chance to talk with her. And if I don't succeed this evening, I'll try again tomorrow."

And that is precisely what she did. She went to Aderonke's house and talked her into coming out for a walk in the evening. While they were on their walk, they met Remi at the edge of the forest.

"Oh, Remi! What a surprise!" Ranti said, as convincingly as she could, "Do come and meet my friend. Aderonke, this is my only and most dear brother, Remi."

"Hello, Aderonke!" Remi said, nodding politely. "I don't think we have met before. Where are you from?"

"Why, Aderonke is from right here in town!" Ranti exclaimed. "She's from the Asala compound, didn't you know?"

"Seriously, Sister, she must have just come to town. I would have known if such a lovely young lady lived here!"

"Oh, no! She's been here in town as long as I can remember. Why, we've been friends for years and years." Ranti turned to Aderonke and asked, "You did live in the capital for a while, didn't you, Aderonke?"

"Yes, we did. But we returned when I was nine. It's been eight years now, you know."

"You've been in this town eight years and hidden yourself the whole time?" Remi asked.

"I don't go out that much," Aderonke said, "but I haven't been hiding. Mostly I stay home with my parents."

"That's nice," Remi said. "That sounds like my kind of young lady!"

"I'm really happy around my house," Aderonke explained. "My parents keep me busy most of the time because I have no sisters."

Ranti suddenly clutched her stomach and yelped, "Oh!"

"What's the matter, Sister?" Remi asked, feigning concern as best he could.

"I don't know. My stomach hurts. Oh, dear! Remi, I think I must go home quickly. I'm afraid I'm going to be sick! I—I'll come back in a few minutes, Aderonke." With this rather weak excuse, Ranti left, and Remi and Aderonke were alone.

"Your dress is stunning," Remi said. (He was not used to making polite conversation with young ladies, and this compliment was the first thing he could think of to say.) "And it matches your beauty, too. You are a lovely young lady."

Aderonke giggled and then said, "You are quite handsome yourself."

"Does my sister visit you often?" Remi asked.

"Well, we don't receive very many visitors," Aderonke said, "but your sister and I have been friends for many years, and we do try to spend some time together when we can."

"I would be very much honored if I could see you once in a while myself," Remi confided. "You are so lovely that just to look at you is a good omen! I think if I had the joy of seeing you in the morning, I would feel fantastic the rest of the day!"

"I am terribly busy, Remi," Aderonke said cautiously. "As I mentioned, my parents do keep me busy, and they don't really encourage me to have visitors."

Remi's heart sank, but Aderonke smiled at him, and he felt better. He proceeded, "If I could see you only a few minutes each day, it would give me great joy."

"It would be almost impossible to see me every day," Aderonke said. "Really, I don't have the opportunity to get out and see people much."

"Oh, Aderonke! Don't you see what it would mean to me? I can feel it—wherever you are, all good things gather around."

"I don't know....We shall have to wait and see."

"I don't mean that you would have to come out here," Remi said. "That would be too much trouble, surely. I could come to your house instead. If I knew where to look, I could get a glimpse of you through the window! Only a glimpse!"

"Remi! That's certainly strange!" Aderonke exclaimed. "It wouldn't be at all safe for you. For one thing, there's my big dog. I don't think he would want someone peeking in my windows. And I know my father certainly wouldn't! You are the brother of my friend, so I don't want you to be bitten or worse! If you were to visit me—and I don't say for a minute that I agree to it—you would have to come to our house, but my parents frown at the idea of men coming over to visit, and I could not do anything that would upset them."

"You are very precious to me, Aderonke," Remi admitted. "I cannot simply forget you. Please believe me when I say I am sincere. I want only to be around you for a short time each day. Can you imagine how happy I am right now just being here with you? I treasure—no, I cherish—this moment, and I will always remember it. O, Providence, if I could be so blessed as to renew such a rare occasion each day, it would feel like being king of all the earth!"

At this eloquent speech, Aderonke smiled such a brilliant smile that poor Remi thought his knees would give out under him.

"Remi, I do want us to be sincere with each other. I think I would like to see you, but I don't know about whether it would be possible. If I were to agree but my parents were to object, what could I do?"

Overflowing with optimism, Remi said, "You never know. You might think your parents would object, but they might not. It's true that they would have the right to turn me away if I were to approach your door, but I would rather take the chance than never know for sure and never see you again."

"We are going out of town tomorrow to visit my aunt. We won't be back for some time," Aderonke said.

"Oh—what can I give you to remember me by while you're away?" Remi asked.

"You need not give me anything, Remi. I shall remember you."

"I'm grateful to you, Aderonke. You know, I can come out with my sister in the future whenever she goes to see you."

"That's true....Of course, you can always go where your sister goes!"

"I would go to any lengths to see you! I will do anything at all that you require!"

"Not that *I* require! Who am I to require anything of you?" Aderonke said playfully.

Remi felt encouraged, and he figured he may as well be brave while he had the chance.

"Don't be like that, now," he said softly, placing Aderonke's hands in his. "You can require anything at all of me."

"I wonder why you want to make friends with me so quickly!" Aderonke said. "You know nothing about me, and looks can be deceitful."

"Not so!" Remi protested. "My sister is the dearest person in the world to me. She wants to have the very best for me, and it was she who told me of your charm. She would never even suggest that I talk to someone of questionable character. Sometimes I think she watches over me as if I were her own child! She says you are a wonderful person. In fact, she talked so much about you that I could hardly wait to meet you. It's a matter of respect. She respects you greatly, and I respect her judgment."

"Ah! So Ranti would make us friends! Does she often make decisions for other people?" Aderonke's words sounded angry, but Remi could see in her eyes that she was only teasing.

"Don't be angry, Aderonke. I just wanted you to know why I am so ready to think well of you. Ranti said you are as sweet as you are beautiful—and what else could I ask for? You are the sweetest and the most beautiful girl I have ever seen! Make any condition at all—I will fulfill it."

"A condition? The condition is that you leave me alone and never dare to see me again!"

"Aderonke! Please be serious. I want to be your friend. I want to be your husband!"

Poor Remi hardly knew whether to laugh at Aderonke's joke or to cry; perhaps it wasn't a joke at all.

At that moment, Ranti came up and said, "Please, Aderonke, treat my brother right. He is just as wonderful as you, but he takes everything so seriously. He may be poor, but look how handsome he is!"

She took her brother's arm and showed off his muscles to Aderonke. "Look at that! He is a paragon of a man! And he doesn't pursue the ladies. Let's see....He's honest, hardworking, dependable—his very word is his oath. Who knows him better than I? And I have never met a finer person than my own brother. If I had to choose a husband, I would want one exactly like him."

"All right," Aderonke joked, "I'll marry him right now. Why not?"

"I'm not kidding!" Remi's sister said. "This is one of those special moments that our whole lives turn on. Can't you be serious just one minute? Truly, I want the best for Remi and the best for you; he is my brother, and you are my friend."

Aderonke's face became serious. Nobody said anything for what seemed to Remi like a few hours. Finally, Remi's sister put her arm around Aderonke's shoulder and rocked her back and forth.

"Never come to my house again!" Aderonke said to Remi.

Aderonke laughed. Ranti laughed, too.

"Never you mind, Remi! She is trying to see how far she can push you! She'll come around. You wait and see."

Bewildered, Remi inquired, "Are you serious, Aderonke, about going out of town?"

"Out of town?" Ranti echoed. "Is that true?"

Aderonke laughed again.

"She's going nowhere!" Ranti assured him. "Has she been this difficult all this time?"

"It's getting late," Aderonke said. "It will be dark in a few minutes, and my mother will worry. I've got to go now."

"All right, so will I see you later on in the evening?" Remi asked.

"You said you wanted to see me once a day!" she answered. "You've not only seen me today, but you've talked to me longer than any young man has ever had the chance! Can't you wait until next week to see me again?"

"No, I can't. Once a day. How about tomorrow?" Remi persisted.

"All right," Aderonke said. "Tomorrow around sunset."

Ranti gave Aderonke a hug, and both girls were laughing as Aderonke started home.

"I wish I knew whether she was teasing me," Remi confessed as soon as Aderonke had left them.

"Yes, she is! Aderonke has never in her life had to deal with anything difficult or serious, and she likes to make jokes. You have to remember that she's never been poor and never had to work a day in her life. Don't you worry—she's going to be your wife! But there are many other men who would like to marry Aderonke, and they're ready to spend a considerable amount of money to get her for a wife. Just be very easy with her, and it will work out. Just you remember that I've known her since she was a skinny, little runt. I know how she thinks." She patted her brother on the cheek and turned with him down the path toward home.

Deep in thought, Remi walked along slowly. *Why was Aderonke such a terrible tease?* he wondered. *I am thinking marriage, and she is acting like a silly girl! Anyone can see she is no longer a child, and she really is as intelligent and delightful as Ranti said.*

*No one could be luckier than I am,* he thought. *I have such a witty sister! I think Aderonke really listens to her, even if she does tease. If Aderonke should actually marry me, our first child will live with Ranti to remind us all how it came about.... Now I've got to get my mother to go through her friends to Aderonke's parents. Young people can get straight to the point, but the older folks have all the formalities to go through—nobody can navigate those like my mother. Aderonke is such a favorite with her parents that they'd give her anything she wanted. If she really wanted to marry me, I think her parents would agree to it....*

*But the other suitors! What in the world can I do to get rid of them? Tenacity and purpose will count here....I hope none of them has a sister like mine! I won't think about their money. And I won't think of myself as poor. I've got to think of myself as the person Aderonke wants to marry, as someone who can change things that need changing. What I can do for myself will matter here. I've got to work hard—harder than ever before—but I'm strong. I've seen people with no hands decide to work with their toes. I've seen deaf people make great music for festivals. I've seen an orphan become chief of the tribe. I would not be the first man to be born into poverty and work his way to wealth! Why should I be one of those who wallow in want and leave this world without any achievements?*

As he walked along in the dusk, Remi's thought pattern became almost like a chant. Over and over, he said the following to himself:

I've got to overcome my disadvantage!
I've got to overcome my limitations!
I can make it; I'm sure I can make it!

I can make it regardless of the obstacles!
I can be richer than all the rich suitors!
I can be richer because I love Aderonke more!
I can be richer because I will sacrifice more!
I can be richer if I strive harder than they!
I am going to strive harder.
I am going to win Aderonke.
I am going to sacrifice more.
I am going to win Aderonke.
I am going to make Aderonke part of my life!
I am going to make Aderonke my wife!

By the time Remi settled down to sleep that night, he had decided to give Aderonke a present: a writing pad and a pen. He would encourage her to write to him. He knew Aderonke was a well-educated young lady, but she had little opportunity to use her skills. This would be an unusual present, one the other suitors would not think of.

And that night Remi dreamed again.

In his dream, Aderonke was at the top of a very steep hill, steeper than any hill Remi had ever seen. Remi was trying to reach her at the top, but so were many other men. The sides of the hill were extremely slippery, as if they were covered with the kind of slimy moss that grows in shallow streams. Anyone who climbed a little way up the hill inevitably slipped back, usually getting bruised in the process, but everyone kept trying.

Remi felt himself slipping. He tried to hold on, and everyone in the valley below him was shouting at him, encouraging him to let go. He could tell they all wanted him to fall back down, but he dug his fingers into the side of the hill and tried to crawl up. The harder he tried, the louder the people shouted. He became increasingly embarrassed that he was crawling instead of walking. He had to get to the top because Aderonke was there.

His arms were aching. His whole body was aching. He could hear in his head his own voice crying with the crowd, "Let go!"

He was about to let go, feeling unable to crawl any farther, when he heard another voice. It was Ranti.

"Hang on!" she cried. "Hang on! Keep going, Remi! I know you can do it! You've got to endure! It's worth it! It's worth it!"

With these words of encouragement, his strength was renewed. He tried again, and this time he felt himself gaining a purchase on the ground. He stopped slipping and began moving forward again. Up and up he climbed. At last, he reached the top. There was Aderonke. She hugged him and kissed him and placed his hands in her own.

But then, of course, Remi woke up again.

All the next day, Remi could think of nothing but Aderonke. In the afternoon, he took some of the money he had saved and went to the little store in the market square. There he bought some blue writing paper and a silver pen. He tucked the rest of the money in his pocket.

Remi went to Aderonke's house just before sunset. Aderonke's big black dog was nowhere to be seen. Neither were her parents anywhere around. Aderonke herself opened the door to Remi.

For the rest of his life, Remi tried to remember what had happened on that visit to Aderonke, but he could not do so. He only knew that he had brought her the gift, stayed nearly an hour, and felt deliriously happy when he left.

And Remi did not wake from a dream this time. This time it was real, and Remi was certain he was the luckiest man in the world.

# TWO

**R**emi's mother, Tohun, decided to approach a go-between for Remi. She set off early one morning to visit her friend Bimpe.

Of course, Tohun did not go straight to Bimpe's house. That would have been terribly rude, and rudeness while on such an important errand could bring only the worst luck. Instead, Tohun spent time greeting everyone around the compound, kneeling before those who were older than she was and extending her best wishes to all.

When Tohun arrived at Bimpe's door, Bimpe called out to her, "Watch your step, Tohun!"

"Ah, you knew who it was," Tohun said with satisfaction. "I hope everything is going well with you!"

"Why, yes, things are going very well. I am grateful that you should ask. Thank you, Tohun. And how are you this morning?"

"Very well myself. How was your recent journey?"

"Ah, it's a long story, Tohun! If I had known what it would have been like, I would have stayed here. I punished myself for nothing!" Bimpe said with a sigh.

"Was she not home?" Tohun asked.

"Oh, she was home. She wouldn't pay me, though."

"What are you going to do?"

"I stopped at her brother's house on my way back and told him about it," Bimpe answered.

"I don't think that will work," Tohun said. "You reported one wicked person to another!"

"What can I do? I have made every attempt to get my payment."

"Well, don't worry too much about it," Tohun said as she picked up a mat that was rolled up in one corner. She took it outside to give it a shake. Dust flew, then she brought the mat in and spread it on the floor. "This is a well-woven mat," Tohun remarked.

"The price was right, too," Bimpe admitted with a laugh.

"Where did you get it?"

"At the market during the rainy season last year. Since then, I've not spread it....You know, I don't believe I noticed how good it was. It's a pretty pattern, too. I had been thinking of buying another, but I haven't had the money."

"Do buy me one, too, the next time you see them," Tohun said. "How much did it cost you?"

"I don't remember for sure. The price would have gone up, no doubt. Come sit on the mat, Tohun. What would you like to eat? I just cooked some soup last night, and the seasoning turned out perfect."

"Don't worry, Bimpe. I'm not hungry."

"Oh, have a taste," Bimpe urged. "Let me warm it up."

"Bimpe, I'd rather not. Please just come and sit by me and let's talk."

"Tohun," her friend said, "this is not like you. What's wrong?"

"Nothing is wrong—rather, it's a matter of joy," Tohun answered.

"If it's a thing of joy, then let me cook!" Bimpe exclaimed. She started a little fire and put the soup on it to heat. "There, now I'm coming, and we can finally talk."

"It's nothing alarming," Tohun began, but then she did not seem to know how to proceed.

"What is it, Tohun?" Bimpe asked. "If it is good news, so much the better to talk about!"

"My son, Remi—he has been talking about the daughter of your friend. Aderonke is her name."

"Yes, Aderonke. I called at their house last night on my way home. Times have changed! No one dares betroth a girl now! Their eyes are on so many men, and whoever they bring in for a husband, that is the person the parents must choose."

"Is it really so? But you get the best choice of oranges if you know someone in charge of oranges," Tohun said.

"You don't have to say anything. I understand. Aderonke is mine, and Remi is mine as well. No one would say I had achieved anything extraordinary if they were to become husband and wife—there's no demarcation between the water and the dye!"

"I know what you are talking about," Tohun said. "I can't even betroth Remi's sister to anyone. It seems the girls make up their minds and do what they will."

"Then you get my point. I was in Aderonke's house one evening, and her mother was telling me that she's worried because all kinds of men have been visiting their house. Aderonke is getting so many presents from them, but she has not told her parents that she has made any choice. Her mother is afraid there is going to be trouble when all these suitors get tired of waiting and when Aderonke chooses one over the others. It looks like trouble either way!"

"I understand that girl is lucky with men," Tohun said.

"That's a fact," Bimpe said, stirring the soup. "Well, I shall see Eli tonight. Who knows? We may say there is no way, but God may say there is a way after all. When I get through talking to her, if it's not dark, I'll stop by to see you."

"Thank you so much, Bimpe. This matter is uppermost in my mind, especially since Remi cannot seem to think of anything else."

"I can understand why," Bimpe said. "Do you want to tell me he is not old enough to be a husband yet? Most of his peers are married already."

Bimpe dished up the soup and set it on the mat between them. The two friends ate from the same bowl as they talked. When they were through eating, Bimpe wrapped some pepper in a leaf and put it in a basket with two yams.

"Here, Tohun, I want you to take these things that I have extra from my journey. And don't you fret about the outcome."

That evening Bimpe visited Aderonke's parents. Aderonke's dog made a dreadful uproar, but Eli chased him off.

"Don't pay any attention to him," she said. "Sometimes he is crazy! Come on in."

"Why, Eli, you look drawn! Are you ill?" Bimpe asked.

Eli paused before answering, "No...not ill."

"There is nothing falling from above that earth cannot contain," Bimpe said.

"There's nothing wrong," Eli said. "Thank you for your gift yesterday. Come into the sitting room—I already spread a mat. Or would you like to come to my room?"

"Let's go to your room. Your daughter's friends would not be so likely to disturb us there."

"You must know what I am going through," Eli said. "Two young men left just now. I wouldn't be surprised if you had seen them on your way here."

"I think I did see someone—two or three men," Bimpe agreed.

"Two came in. Who can tell? Maybe there was a third who didn't come in. I am so overwhelmed with people! My mind is full. I'm glad you came. I think I would have gone to see you had you not come."

"Do try to relax, Eli. I always tell you to be full of prayer. The one who does not plant corn plants something else!"

"It's this matter of Aderonke. I can't understand what's happening, but I can tell you this. We have bought many things for Aderonke, and Aderonke is not working for anyone, but now we have presents all over this house—presents that we did not buy and that Aderonke did not buy for herself! She does not steal, and our money has not been touched. Now where do you think all these presents are coming from, Bimpe?"

"Ah, Eli, she is still young! She is still a child who will take presents from anyone. Have her tell you who gave her which presents so that when she finally makes her choice, the other items can be returned."

"What would you like me to cook for you?" Eli asked. "I have not eaten lunch yet."

"Lunch!" Bimpe exclaimed. "Eli, it is already sunset! No wonder you look so drawn! You have had nothing to eat!"

"I haven't been very hungry lately," Eli replied.

"Rest your mind, Eli. Nothing will happen. Aderonke did not ask anyone to give her anything. They *chose* to give her the presents. Now you get something to eat."

Just then the dog barked. "Let me go see who is there," Eli said. When she got to the door, a young man prostrated himself in front of her and asked if Aderonke was home.

"She is not here," Eli said, exasperated. The young man left as quickly as he had come, and Eli fixed a bowl of stew for herself and her friend.

"It was another of Aderonke's suitors," Eli said. "I don't think I have seen this one before."

"You know, Eli, Tohun came to see me this morning. She told me her son, Remi, is interested in Aderonke. We spoke at some length. She and you are both my dear friends; Aderonke and Remi are mine as well."

"I did explain to you how these boys were coming to see Aderonke," Eli replied. "You saw a little of it."

"I see what you mean, but my friend Tohun could not tell me this without me coming to see you."

"Our children do not take after us!" Eli said sadly. "During our time, we would not have opened our mouth to talk to men!"

"Our time is a long time ago," Bimpe answered.

"As much as I would like to tell my daughter which suitor to marry, she would hardly listen to me. We will support whatever choice she makes. We should not be indebted to people we will later regret. You know, I am not denying you anything—if you can talk her into it, I have no objection at all."

"It looks to me," Bimpe said, "as if she cannot make up her mind. The men keep coming, and they are willing to give her presents. You should get her to tell you who gave her what, though, so that each one can be compensated when she marries someone else."

"I hope no one hurts her," Eli confided. "These young men are proud, and I am certain some of them are going to be angry when Aderonke marries someone else. After all, she can marry only one man! And we have only this one daughter! You do not know how much we longed to have more children, but only this one was apportioned to us! What would I do were someone to hurt my only child?" At this thought, tears filled Eli's eyes.

"You don't have to weep, Eli," Bimpe said kindly. "This only child will have many children herself, you wait and see. You have already wept so much that you look haggard, and too much weeping makes one sick."

Eli dried her tears and tried to smile before saying, "I am sorry, Bimpe. I have been so worried for my child. Tell me. How is Tohun's business now? Is it still the same with her?"

"It is the same as ever. They are terribly poor, with the whole family working hard. His father is usually on the farm, although they hardly scratch enough from it to eat. Tohun and the children spend long hours cutting and marketing firewood, and Remi goes out to the farm, too. They don't live an easy life. Sometimes I think of myself as poor—but not when I remember Tohun and her family."

"Tohun is the daughter of a wonderful person."

"She is like that herself," Bimpe replied. "Unfortunately, though, kindness is not the same as good luck."

"Please greet her for me," Eli said. "Let her know that Aderonke seems unable to make up her mind. Her face is turned toward many men. Meanwhile, I will see what I can do about sorting out all these gifts."

On the way home, Bimpe stopped to see Tohun as she had promised. The two friends went to talk in Tohun's room for privacy, but just as they settled down on the mat, Tohun called for Remi. "You can't shave a man's hair in his absence," she remarked.

Bimpe told Tohun and Remi all that had happened at Eli's house. "She has said that she and her husband will not choose a husband for Aderonke. Aderonke will choose for herself. The problem is that she has not chosen, and there are some very impatient suitors who have given an incredible number of presents to her. Eli fears trouble ahead, and I think she may be right."

"Do you mean to say," Tohun asked hopefully, "that they would accept Remi for their son-in-law despite his material poverty?"

"Yes!" Bimpe answered triumphantly. "If Aderonke had not received so many presents from so many men and if they did not fear trouble ahead, it might not be so. But they are so worried that they simply want Aderonke to choose a suitor—anyone at all. She just needs to choose someone! And Eli is kindly disposed to your son for the kindness of your own mother to hers. Then, too, she is my friend, and because I have recommended Remi, she will think highly of him. She knows that I understand her problem and that I fully realize how much she loves her daughter."

"I thought she had forgotten the kindness of my mother," Tohun admitted.

"No, she remarked on it herself. I think she has feared that you would be embarrassed to be around her, that you might think she looked down on you for your poverty. But that is not so. She is only a woman worried about her child, just as you are. I think she would like to see you, Tohun."

Tohun sighed and turned to her son. She said, "You have the whole story, Remi. I am sure Eli would not lightly treat what Bimpe told her, but there is no solution right now. We will have to be patient. Many young women are as pretty as Aderonke, should you not want to wait."

"I understand what you mean," Remi replied, "but I think we can look at this positively. Aderonke has to be someone's wife one day, and I am not afraid of competition. One who is lucky and hardworking always wins, and I think I will be lucky in this. Did her mother not already say that if Aderonke chooses me, then I may be her husband? We had thought her parents would stand in the way, but that is not so; therefore, I think the prize will go to me!"

"You are sure of yourself!" Tohun said, laughing.

"If I do not try, I will not win!" Remi declared. "I will have to champion my own cause and not become discouraged. Later I will need help in making all the arrangements, but it looks now as if what I must do is simply convince Aderonke to marry me!"

"You see, Tohun," Bimpe said, "his mind is made up! Let's not discourage him. We can assist him with prayer, and if he is the right man for her, no one will be able to prevent it. And if we don't help him now, he'll never forget it." Bimpe put her arms around Remi's neck and gave him a quick hug. "You are right, Remi, you are right. Look at my face. Your mother and I will do our best. If Aderonke is your choice, then that is the way it will be."

"Thank you, Bimpe," Remi said. "I am so grateful to you. Now I must go see what I can do about this myself."

After Remi had left, Bimpe told Tohun, "Even while I was there, several men came to see Aderonke. He can talk to her himself."

"He certainly can act on his own," Tohun said. "I did not know he had gone to see Aderonke nor that he had given her a gift. Ranti told me this morning. I think I have no more control over Remi than Eli has over Aderonke! The big problem is all those suitors. Which one will Aderonke choose, and what kind of trouble will there be when she has finally made her choice?"

Aderonke's town was a small port, a fishing village that had grown somewhat to allow for trade by sea.

Several months ago, the captain of a boat berthed at the dock had walked into town. Impressively dressed in his official uniform, he spied Aderonke on the main street.

Although Aderonke's town was not much more than a village, Aderonke herself was really a spectacular young lady. The captain, like so many other men, was overwhelmed with her beauty.

Of course, this captain had been in town many times before. He knew every little port on his regular routes—in the dark as well as in the daylight—and had never been lost in all his life. But on this occasion, he decided that he was lost and needed Aderonke's help to find his way.

"Excuse me, young lady," he said politely. "Can you direct me to the pub?"

"There are two pubs, sir," Aderonke answered. "One of them is over there near the dock, and the other is just up the street here."

"Thank you," the captain said. "Perhaps you would be so kind as to accompany me to the one up the street? I am quite new in town and am afraid I have gotten lost somehow."

Aderonke hesitated and then said, "Well, I am walking in this direction anyway. Come with me, and I will show you."

When they arrived at the pub, the captain addressed Aderonke again. "Thank you so much, young lady.

It has been a pleasure to walk with you. As you can see, I have no companions at the moment. Perhaps you would share a drink with me before you go on your way? No doubt you know the bar owner—surely he is a friend of your father?"

The sailor had spoken wisely. If Aderonke's father were indeed the bar owner's friend, Aderonke would not be afraid to go into the pub. And if she refused, there was always the chance that he might say something about how a young lady had seemed afraid to enter the pub belonging to her father's friend!

*Well,* Aderonke thought, *I will be here only a few minutes. And it is true that I know everyone here. This seems to be a fine sort of gentleman—educated and very well-mannered. What harm could it do?*

Inside the pub, the captain told Aderonke about how he enjoyed sailing to the major ports of the world. (This was exaggerated, but in Aderonke's eyes, the captain appeared honorable and trustworthy. She could hardly be expected to know that he really traveled only back and forth along the coast for a few hundred miles!) He told her how he could buy anything from any country in the world, and he claimed to know where everything was the cheapest. The ports of the world had glittering entertainment for visitors like himself and his friends. The sea was beautiful, and its islands were more beautiful still. And the food! No one could imagine all the wonderful food at the seaports of the world! Why, he had not yet tasted even half of the cuisine the world had to offer!

Aderonke was enthralled by his captivating tales.

"Have you ever been on board a ship before?" he asked in a tone indicating that he assumed such an intelligent and lovely young lady had probably been on board many times.

"Never! I have never even been in a little boat before," she confessed.

"Why, what wonderful luck!" the captain said. "This is a special day aboard my ship. The guests of the senior officers will attend a great feast because an important official is coming by for an inspection. Would you care to accompany me? I should be delighted to have your company, and I do believe that somewhere among the treasures we have stored on the ship I can find a small gift to thank you for your kindness to me."

Aderonke was not, of course, a worldly, sophisticated young lady. In fact, she was something of an overgrown child. It did not occur to her that this handsome captain had in mind anything other than to show her his beautiful ship; it also never crossed her mind that taking a present from him might in some way obligate her to him.

"Could I be back before sunset?" she asked.

"Why, of course," the captain said agreeably. "Naturally a young lady of your breeding needs to be home before it grows dark. I assure you that I will take very good care of you."

"Oh, thank you!" Aderonke said. "I know I shall have a lovely time."

As they walked toward the dock, the captain told Aderonke more about his work. "You know, some sailors must leave their families for long periods of time—in fact, our men do that, too. But the officers are able to take their wives along. I will show you my cabin....I have no wife as yet, but I have plenty of room should I decide to marry. If you have never seen such a thing, I think you will like it. It's really like a house right there aboard the ship."

And it was exactly as the captain had said. His quarters were large and beautiful, with lots of polished wood and heavy furniture. Aderonke had never seen anything like it. The dinner was delicious; Aderonke had never tasted such savory foods. And all the officers were resplendent in their fancy uniforms. The important person from the shipping line made a brief speech, and because Aderonke was the special guest of the captain, everyone paid a great deal of attention to her. When she started home just before sunset, she was full of heady dreams about distant ports and the marvelous life a sailor's wife must lead.

The ship was docked for almost a week longer than it was scheduled to because some goods had not yet arrived, and the captain decided to use the extra time to make small repairs. Every evening he paid Aderonke a visit, and every evening he brought her a gift from some faraway place. And Aderonke visited the ship, or at least came down to the dock to watch the sailors at their work, nearly every day.

Eventually the ship sailed away. But sometimes there was a gift for Aderonke sent in by post or by another ship, and sometimes there was a letter describing some adventure in a distant port.

Two months later, the ship came back. And this is how Aderonke acquired one of her most ardent suitors.

Aderonke's jealous friends giggled together whenever they saw the fine captain. They mocked Aderonke and whispered nasty words sbout him in her ears. Aderonke, however, was too innocent to know of jealousy. She thought perhaps there was something wrong with the sailor.

Aderonke's friends made up this song, and they sang it together where Aderonke could hear them:

> If you marry a sailor,
> If you marry a sailor,
> If you marry a sailor,
> Know for sure that

He may be mad at you one day
And drown you at sea!
If you marry a sailor!

Poor Aderonke, who really liked the sailor, could not make up her mind about what to do. Should she marry him and go off to sea and visit the great ports of the world? Were they right that if she made him angry, he would drown her? What should she do? But because she had never had to make a single decision for herself all her life and because everything had always turned out well for her, Aderonke simply did nothing.

On another occasion, Aderonke had gone to the pharmacist for some medicine for her father. Aderonke had never been in the pharmacy before, and she was fascinated by the rows and rows of jars, bottles, boxes, and other packages. The pharmacist, however, was fascinated with Aderonke.

The prescription slip listed Aderonke's father's name and address as well as four separate medications. Of these four medicines, three were not effective by themselves; they must be taken in combination with the fourth. As is true all over the world, the prescription was written in a sort of doctor's code—and the handwriting was terrible. Only a pharmacist can read a prescription!

As a result, the pharmacist gave Aderonke only three packages of medicine, all wrapped up neatly so that they wouldn't get dirty if they were accidentally dropped. He tied the packages together with a string to make them easier to carry, and he thanked Aderonke for her business.

Aderonke's father was not home when she returned, so she put the package where he would find it and went about doing other things. How surprised she was when the pharmacist came to her door later that afternoon!

"Hello, ma'am," the pharmacist said. "I found this other medication in the shop. I believe my assistant forgot to wrap it with the others. It is the one that makes the others effective, and I would not want your father to have to do without it even for one day."

"Why, thank you so much!" Aderonke said. "I am certainly glad you brought it, for this medicine is extremely important. My father usually gets it in the city, but he hasn't been there for sometime. You are very kind."

"No problem at all," the pharmacist said. "I hope your father has not been ill."

"Yes," Aderonke answered, "as a matter of fact, he has been rather ill recently. My mother said I must be certain to get his medicine because when he takes it, he is fine, but when he stops taking it, he gets quite sick."

"I am sorry to hear that," the pharmacist said. "I will stop by tomorrow evening to make certain he has everything he needs. Perhaps I can make some recommendation if he is still feeling ill."

"Thank you again. I know my father will appreciate that."

When her father came home, he was very glad to see that the medicine had been procured. He took it at once, and within a short time, he was feeling much better. By the next morning, he seemed to be his old self again. This made Aderonke exceedingly happy, for she loved her parents greatly.

When the pharmacist visited the house the next evening, Aderonke was quick to tell him how the medicine had helped her father.

"And I would never have known about the fourth bottle if you had not been so kind as to bring it," she said. "I am forever grateful to you. With no doctor here in town, it's wonderful to have a pharmacist who is as thoughtful and wise as you."

"I think," the pharmacist said, "if I may say so, that the trouble with your father must have to do with his heart. Is that correct?"

"I do not know," Aderonke said honestly. "My father has never told me. Why do you ask?"

"I have something in the shop that is ideal for people with heart trouble. It would not hurt him if his heart is not his problem, but it serves to strengthen the heart. Would you like me to bring some of it by tomorrow?" the pharmacist offered.

"Thank you. That would be very kind of you," Aderonke replied.

Thus, little by little, the pharmacist gained Aderonke's favor and her trust. Because she cared so much about her father, she looked up to the pharmacist as someone whose concern and knowledge were most welcome. Little by little, the pharmacist began to plant in Aderonke's mind an idea of what it would be like to become the wife of a pharmacist.

The pharmacist never actually mentioned Aderonke's wealth, of course, but it was clear to Aderonke that with a little help from her parents, they could own the largest pharmacy for many miles around. Of course, if they owned such a large drugstore, they would also enjoy a large house—much larger than the quarters of a sea captain, for example.

He involved Aderonke in his business planning, asking her advice regarding the arrangement of the products in his shop as well as other matters. Quite naturally, Aderonke was flattered that he sought her opinions.

Aderonke's friends, who made fun of the sea captain because they were jealous, were actually alarmed at all the attention the pharmacist was paying her. When Aderonke told them how the pharmacist had brought the fourth bottle of medicine and how much better her father had gotten that night, they quickly figured out that the pharmacist must have kept the bottle out of the package on purpose. But, of course, Aderonke would not hear of it because she believed that the pharmacist's intentions were pure.

Aderonke's friends also knew the pharmacist was having business trouble. One of them had heard from her father that the pharmacist was dishonest and that he was losing customers because of it. People waited to have their prescriptions filled until someone was taking a trip to the city because some of his drugs were tainted. But it did no good to say such things to Aderonke; she was convinced that the pharmacist was a hero.

Then again, Aderonke's friends could see what would happen if the pharmacist married Aderonke. Aderonke was an only child, and her parents doted on her. They would certainly settle their property on the pharmacist, who would then be rich. It was obvious to Aderonke's friends that he was after her family's money.

Aderonke's friends finally decided to take drastic action. One day when the pharmacist came to visit Aderonke, they came along, too. And together they sang this song:

If you marry a pharmacist,
If you marry a pharmacist,
If you marry a pharmacist,
Know for sure that
He may be mad at you one day
And splash acid on you!
If you marry a pharmacist!

He was furious. Not only had it crossed his mind that if he married Aderonke, he would acquire all her parents' property, but he had also realized that if he should find her an unpleasant wife, he had all sorts of medications in his shop that would just as easily rid him of her as they had won her in the first place! Nevertheless, the pharmacist was not about to give up. Aderonke was both rich and beautiful, so he would be back.

One of the people Aderonke saw every day was the police officer. Everyone in her neighborhood knew the police officer well; he had grown up in the village and lived near his beat. His sisters were friendly with Aderonke (though they were was not among those who were given to singing about Aderonke's suitors), and his father was an important man in town.

Of course, this police officer came by Aderonke's house several times each day. But more and more, his visits seemed to occur at times when Aderonke's parents were not at home. And more and more, he found reasons to stop for a moment and talk with Aderonke.

There was no question that the police officer looked handsome in his uniform—no matter how hot the day, his creases were always perfect and his buttons shiny. Because the police know everything there is to know and because his father is an important person, he knew all the gossip for miles and miles around. It was also advantageous to be friendly with a police officer. After all, most people tended to distrust the police because they could put you in jail, but if the police officer was your friend, you had nothing to worry about!

One day when her parents were not home, Aderonke was startled by loud knocking at her door. Her big black dog was not barking, though. *Who could that be?* she wondered.

It was the police officer. The dog was not barking because the police officer was scratching its ears; they seemed to understand each other very well and had become good friends in the course of all the police officer's rounds.

"Hello," Aderonke said. "What are you banging on the door about?"

"Oh, Aderonke!" the police officer said. "I'm so glad to see you are all right! Are your parents home?"

"No, did you want to speak to my father?" Aderonke asked.

"No, I was just hoping there was someone here with you. Two criminals escaped from the district jail, and they are known to be quite dangerous. I tracked them to this area but have lost sight of their trail again. I am worried they might hurt you."

"Oh!" Aderonke said, her eyes wide. "How dreadful! What should I do?"

"I will escort you to your aunt's house. Are there people home at her house? You can stay there until your parents come home."

Aderonke gratefully took the police officer's arm and went with him to her aunt's house. Of course, when her parents came home that evening, they were appropriately grateful to the police officer, who stopped by just to make sure everything was okay. From then on, Aderonke's parents looked favorably on the police officer, although whether they ever thought of him as a suitor for their daughter is questionable. Aderonke now thought the police officer was quite brave.

The only thing wrong with Aderonke's opinion of the police officer was that it was based on somewhat faulty information. The police officer may or may not have been brave. That was an open question,

as he had never had occasion to find out. But he
certainly had not rescued Aderonke from any
criminals, dangerous or otherwise. In fact, he had
not chased any criminals on that day or any other.
Indeed, two criminals were missing from the district
jail, but they had taken ship for parts unknown three
days previously.

In short, the police officer had lied. He may have
lied because he really was out of his mind in love
with Aderonke and wanted to appear a hero in her
eyes, but he lied nevertheless.

Over the next few weeks, Aderonke could hardly
be blamed for considering what it would be like to
be married to a police officer. It was true that some
people would have nothing whatsoever to do with
police officers, perhaps out of fear that the police
officers might put them in jail, but her own friends
surely would not cease to be her friends on that
account. Would they? And although her own family
was both well-known and wealthy, if she married
the police officer, her father-in-law would be one of
the most important men in the whole district.

Aderonke's friends had, of course, heard about
the escaped criminals, and when Aderonke told
them about her "rescue" by the police officer, they
did not know he had been lying. But because they
were very much in the habit of making fun of Aderonke's suitors by this time, they invented a song
about the police officer as well:

If you marry a police officer,
If you marry a police officer,
If you marry a police officer,
Know for sure that
He may be mad at you one day
And put you in jail!
If you marry a police officer!

Her friends were now getting to the point at which they argued among themselves about which of the suitors was the worst, and sometimes they carried out these arguments in Aderonke's presence. "Police officers are really dangerous people," one of them would say, and another would answer, "Sailors are notoriously untrustworthy." A third would remind the others, "The pharmacist is a fraud," and then someone would mention, "There is a farmer, too, but who wants to be married to a farmer if she could marry a professional man?" The arguments seemed to go on forever. All the while, Aderonke's suitors continued to visit. She continued receiving presents from them and still seemed unable to make up her mind.

The friends happened to be arguing at Aderonke's house one day, and their argument caused a kidnapping.

# THREE

"That sea captain, or whatever he is, is no good for Aderonke!" one of the friends exclaimed.

Aderonke was right there listening, but for all her friends paid attention to her, she may as well have been a wall.

"Fine!" another shouted. "So do you think she should marry the pharmacist? He is nothing but a fraud who is after her money!"

"Well, do you expect her to marry a police officer?" the first friend asked. "His father may be an important man, but a police officer is just not the sort for a well-mannered young lady like Aderonke."

"Well, then," a third friend said, "she certainly can't marry a farmer. Her family has progressed beyond that sort of thing, and she needs to marry better than that."

"I don't see what you're complaining about!" the first friend yelled. "After all, Aderonke doesn't seem to mind a peasant. Why should she care about whether a farmer is good enough for her?"

"A peasant!" the others exclaimed in unison.

"Yes, a peasant. I've seen her more than once with him, and the way she hangs on him, you'd think they were ready to discuss the details of their wedding arrangements yesterday. At least he can't give her expensive presents that she'll have to return!"

Her friends were surprised when Aderonke spoke. "Remi is a peasant today because his grandmother was too generous to mine! And he *has* given me a present—something I like better than anything anyone else has given me!"

Aderonke's friends began to talk all at once, and they were chattering like monkeys when the police officer dropped by.

The police officer had never heard of Remi, but he quickly understood the gist of the conversation.

"Who is this fellow?" he inquired just as Aderonke's parents returned.

"What fellow?" Aderonke's father asked.

"This peasant," the police officer stated flatly.

The pharmacist came by at that moment to visit Aderonke's father and see how his health was improving. (Of course, he really wanted to see Aderonke, but with her mischievous friends around, he thought this not a good time for courting.)

"What peasant?" the pharmacist asked.

"What are you doing here?" the police officer asked, looking fiercely at the pharmacist.

The pharmacist drew himself up and said huffily, "I am visiting one of my customers to make certain his medication is satisfactory."

At this, Aderonke's friends burst out laughing and began to sing their song—all the verses, beginning with the one about the pharmacist.

"I protest this nonsense!" the pharmacist shouted indignantly.

"These young women ought to be hauled in and imprisoned for being public nuisances!" the police officer said, gritting his teeth and trying to look official.

Aderonke laughed so hard that she could hardly stand up.

Aderonke's mother wrung her hands and abruptly retreated to her own room.

Aderonke's father said, "That is enough! I am extremely tired, as I have been out on business all day. I am sorry that I cannot offer you my hospitality. Will everyone please leave now?"

The girls hurried out the door, but Aderonke's father had to escort the police officer and the pharmacist, saying soothing things all the while. When they had left, he mopped his brow with his big white handkerchief. Something would have to be done about these suitors.

The next day, Remi was on his way to Aderonke's house to visit her when he was accosted by the pharmacist.

"So! You are the peasant who wants to get his dirty hands on Aderonke!" he cried mercilessly.

"I have better manners than some people," Remi replied, "and my hands are clean."

"You are nothing but a filthy peasant, and you have no right to see Aderonke at all!" the pharmacist shouted.

"That is for Aderonke and her parents to say," Remi responded calmly.

"That is for me to say!" the pharmacist snarled. And with that, he lunged at Remi and wrestled him to the ground.

Remi was so astounded at this sudden attack that it took him a moment to react, but when he finally did, the pharmacist found himself lying on his back in the dirt with a cracked rib, a bloody nose, and a badly swollen black eye.

Remi pulled the pharmacist to his feet and said, "Now, then, what was for you to say?"

The pharmacist was not only a fraud; he was stupid. He attacked Remi again.

But Remi was ready for him this time. Once again the pharmacist lay in the dirt, and one of his feet stuck out at an odd angle.

A few of the neighbors came to see what the fuss was about, and one of them helped the pharmacist back to his shop. Because Remi had gotten a bit dirty during this fight, however short it may have been, he decided to go home and clean up before proceeding to Aderonke's house.

Another of Aderonke's suitors, a seller of palm wine, was among the bystanders. "So you are the famous peasant suitor!" he shouted in disgust. "I think you need to be discouraged."

Unfortunately for Remi, the palm-wine seller was a much better fighter than the pharmacist. In the next two or three minutes, Remi got knocked around quite a bit. But within five minutes, it was all over. The palm-wine seller was sitting on the ground, holding his head. He felt so dizzy that he couldn't stand up.

This time when Remi tried to go home, no one bothered him.

Aderonke's suitors were not likely to cooperate with one another in anything, but things were a bit different on this occasion. The two who had been badly beaten by Remi got together to discuss the matter.

The pharmacist was a coward to begin with, and he was not about to put himself in any additional danger from Remi. The palm-wine seller was no coward, and he was a fairly good fighter himself, but he had decided that alone, he was no match for Remi. They could not gang up on him because the pharmacist refused to get personally involved.

They thought of complaining to the police officer so that Remi would be put in jail for disturbing the peace, but there were too many witnesses to say that the envious suitors themselves were to blame for starting the fights. Finally they decided to hire some thugs to get rid of Remi once and for all. Then Aderonke would not marry a peasant. The pharmacist, of course, thought she would marry him. And the palm-wine seller, quite naturally, thought she would marry him.

Between them, the palm-wine seller and the pharmacist knew practically everyone for miles around, and it did not take them long to find four thugs who were willing to kidnap Remi and "take him where he won't bother Aderonke again." No one said anything about killing him, but everyone knew that was what was expected.

As Remi returned home from Aderonke's house one evening, these four thugs stepped out from behind some bushes, knocked Remi over the head, and dragged him away. They took him to the dock, put him in a little boat, and rowed out to sea. When they were a good distance from land, they dumped him overboard.

It wasn't long before the thugs merrily drank up their payment at the local pub. Meanwhile, the pharmacist and the palm-wine seller dreamed of Aderonke.

Remi, however, was not dead. Because the thugs used no lights when they pulled out to sea for fear of being discovered, they were unaware that Remi had recovered consciousness. Remi held his breath whenever they touched him so that they would think he was already dead from the blow to his head.

Remi knew they would kill him if they thought there was any life left in him, so he did a marvelous job of playing dead. The trick worked, and the thugs were none the wiser.

When the thugs were out of earshot in their rowboat, Remi started swimming for shore, aiming diagonally across the bay to avoid his attackers. He made for a rocky headland that was some distance away, but his swimming was not as good as usual because he was still feeling the effects of the blow on his head, not to mention the fights the day before.

It was a moonless night, which would not have been bad except that the sky was overcast. Whether it was the confusion in his head or the almost pitch-darkness, Remi missed the headland and actually swam out toward the open sea. It was a long time before he realized his mistake, and by then he was terribly tired.

The sea was fairly calm, so Remi turned over on his back to float a few minutes and try to think about what to do next. He knew he could not last much longer alone in the open sea, and it was quite a while until dawn. He could not be a long distance from the shore, but he dared not waste his energies on a wrong guess about the direction he should take.

Remi was startled when he bumped into something solid. What was it? A boat? He heard no one and saw no outline, however faint, in the dark. Gingerly, he felt for the object again. There it was! He grabbed a hold of the side of it.

The object seemed to be a sizable piece of driftwood—apparently a young tree that had been uprooted in some storm. It offered little support, but Remi held on gratefully, glad of any help. The tree had not been in the water long because it was still covered with leaves. Surely he could not be very far from land. All he would have to do is be patient until sunrise so that he could get his bearings.

Remi may have dozed part of the rest of the night; it seemed to him that he had not really been in the water for so many hours when the sky began to lighten. When he got a good look at his life raft, he discovered that it was indeed a small tree, and as he looked about, he saw that there were other small trees and some branches nearby. They were spread along the surface of the sea almost in a line. He hoisted himself up as well as he could and strained his eyes to find the shore.

It was nowhere to be seen.

The sun, of course, was rising in the east, and in a general sort of way land could be said to be somewhere toward the east, but if he had drifted far during the night, he might swim all day and still not reach shore. Perhaps he should swim eastward in hopes of being seen by fishermen or other coastal traffic.

Remi began to swim toward the sun. But the harder he swam, the less distance he seemed to cover. Whenever he stopped and looked back to gauge his progress, he discovered that his little tree was not far away. In fact, either the entire patch of driftwood was following him or he was going nowhere at all. He realized that he must be caught in one of those currents that run up and down in the ocean like great rivers.

It occurred to Remi that sometimes ships traveled such currents, so he might be seen by some merchant vessel or pleasure craft during the day. On the other hand, at night his position would be perilous, as he was likely to be run down before anyone saw him.

And he was thirsty. He could not drink seawater, so from time to time he chewed on some of the leaves still clinging to the driftwood. He could think of nothing else to do but wait until he spotted either land or a ship.

By evening, Remi's spirits were low indeed. He had seen one merchant vessel, but it was a long way off, and his shouting and splashing about (he had even tried waving a small branch) had no effect. He was hungry, sore, and tired, and he felt as if his skin were being pickled. Most of all, he was thirsty. However, the sun was going down. At least the heat would not be so terrible now.

Remi may have slept some that night while floating along, or he may have fainted, or he may have been delirious. But again the night did not seem as long as he had thought it would.

There was no question that he was growing weaker. Any attempt to break out of the current would simply use the last of his strength, and Remi was not foolish. He tried to conserve his energy, although he occasionally swam back and forth in a small area to drag some of the smaller branches to the little tree and weave them together for a tad more buoyancy. It was hardly a raft, and he could not climb up on it, but it did offer some support. Other than this, he conserved his energy as much as possible. When the current approached land or when he saw a ship close by, he wanted to have the strength to make his bid for safety.

Unfortunately, the current seemed to be traveling steadily toward the northwest. This was definitely away from any land he knew, but Remi reasoned that his own was not the only country in the world. If one went far enough, one was bound to come to something. The problem would be staying alive long enough to get somewhere.

Remi saw neither ship nor land that day. And as the sun sank, his heart nearly sank with it. His lips were cracked and bleeding, and he knew that his mind was not working as well as it should. If he did not find rescue tomorrow, he would most likely die at sea—and all for Aderonke!

That night Remi may have stayed awake, or he may have slept, but he certainly dreamed.

In his dream, he could not see himself except for his hands and feet, and he hardly felt like himself. He was holding a wreath of flowers composed of great red and yellow blooms of a kind he had never seen before. There were flowers all over the ground, and he could hear chanting.

As he listened more closely to the chanting, he realized it was his own voice. The chant mentioned something about Aderonke, but he could not clearly make out the words.

His hands lifted the wreath and then put it on something made of stone. Petals fell all around it. He felt the petals under his feet, but then they changed to sand.

"Aderonke, Aderonke!" he cried.

And as he looked up over the wreath, Aderonke came out of the sea. She was covered with shining seaspray, and she held out her arms to him.

"Aderonke!" he called again.

But when he did so, he got a mouthful of water and woke up choking.

# FOUR

**A**deronke's family was in an uproar, and this was why.

The four thugs who thought they had gotten rid of Remi had gotten thoroughly drunk on their earnings. It wasn't long before they started bragging in the local pub. They were so drunk that no one paid much attention to them at the time, but the next day—and the next—when Remi was nowhere to be found, people remembered the thugs bragging in the pub.

One detail the thugs mentioned in their boasting was how the pharmacist had paid them a great deal of money. So when people began to ask questions about Remi, they naturally took those questions to the pharmacist. The pharmacist, of course, protested complete ignorance of the affair and reminded his neighbors that drunken thugs were not respectable. He also pointed out that if the thugs were capable of killing someone, they would certainly not balk at lying. The palm-wine seller who had conspired with the pharmacist thought it best to argue that the pharmacist was undoubtedly right and that if the thugs had indeed done Remi in, they had done it entirely on their own.

The police officer was, of course, informed. From his point of view, this meant that Remi was out of the way and so was the pharmacist. He arrested the pharmacist for questioning, all the time proclaiming that he didn't for a moment believe him guilty of such a crime. He claimed he was just taking the pharmacist into "protective custody" until the real culprit could be found so that the neighbors would not take the law into their own hands. He launched a search for the thugs, who had prudently left town, although no one actually ever saw the police officer looking for anyone.

Once the pharmacist was under suspicion, so were all of Aderonke's other suitors, including the police officer himself. Each suitor felt that getting married to Aderonke would serve as proof that she and her parents were convinced of his innocence. Presumably this would make all the neighbors believe him innocent as well.

Unfortunately, this put Aderonke's family under terrible strain. The suitors now demanded even more of their time, doubling the gifts and making a constant nuisance of themselves. Aderonke, who had previously enjoyed all the attention, did not like this at all. She worried about Remi, and she became convinced that he was dead. Because he was dead, he glowed more brightly in her mind. Remi had certainly been the most truly ardent of her suitors. He had been willing to compete with wealthy and prominent men for her attention, relying only on the strength of his love for her. He had surely loved her more than any of the others! She should have chosen him, and now, because she had hesitated, he was dead!

In addition to feeling guilty, Aderonke felt harassed. She could see the strain her parents were under. Being a good-hearted girl, she felt sorry that they should be suffering on her account. She was also tired of stumbling over gifts she really did not want—after all, her own father could quite well afford to give her anything she desired—and of not being able to go outside her own door without being set upon by her suitors.

In short, Aderonke was tired of the game that only a few days before had been so much fun. And if Aderonke was tired of it, her poor parents were nearly beside themselves.

Like everyone else in the village, Bimpe heard all about this situation. She was heartbroken at the loss of Remi and spent much of her time trying to comfort Remi's mother and sister. After nearly two weeks, she found an opportunity to visit Eli.

When Bimpe had gotten safely past all the suitors and the big black dog (who gave her less trouble than the young men), she settled down on a mat to listen to Eli's troubles.

"Bimpe, I cannot tell you," Eli said. "I cannot make you understand what we are going through. Did you see all those suitors standing around?"

"I certainly did," Bimpe answered. "I thought I would never get in the door because of them. I had no idea there were so many!"

"I think some of them are friends of the suitors, or they're just curious. We have become a sight for everyone to see now. If Remi has been murdered—may Providence make it not so!—it is because of Aderonke. We are notorious!"

"My poor friend!"

"And that is not all. Aderonke blames herself, and I must admit she was such a child and seemed to be enjoying having so much attention. If she had only made a choice earlier!"

Bimpe murmured sympathetically.

"But now she sees that this is her fault. And, of course, she won't marry any of these young men."

"But why not? Surely she does not want something similar to happen again?" Bimpe asked bewildered.

"No, of course not. But she thinks that any of the suitors could have hired those thugs, and she does not want to marry him for fear of being murdered herself one day. Additionally, she has decided that Remi was the only one of her suitors who was truly sincere, and she adamantly refuses to marry anyone else!" At this revelation, Eli burst into tears.

"Not marry!" Bimpe yelped. "But that is unheard of! What sort of foolish notions does that girl have?"

Eli sniffled loudly and continued, "I just don't know, Bimpe. She believes all the other suitors want to marry her because she is wealthy and pretty, but she knows Remi wanted to marry her because he loved her and would cherish her always. Now that she cannot have Remi, she will have no one. She spends all her time in her room crying or staring into space. Whatever can I do with her?"

"Well," Bimpe answered slowly, "she may be right about the suitors. She is certainly right that at least one of them must have hired those thugs. Remi had no other enemies than the suitors themselves because he was so kind and helpful. And they could not have robbed him. Everyone knows Remi had no money at all. If I were Aderonke, I would not want to take a chance on marrying a murderer either!"

"But she must marry somebody!" Eli exclaimed.

"Of course, of course...but Aderonke is still young, and she has suffered a terrible loss. I think Remi would have made her the best husband—you know that, because we have talked about it before—and she seems to realize it. It's understandable that she is sad because she believes it was her fault he was attacked. How can she think of marrying now? She needs time to get over her sorrow, and then she will be all right."

Eli sighed deeply. "I'm sure you are right, Bimpe. But how can she have time when we have all these suitors outside the house? We have no privacy at all. We can hardly think, let alone decide on a good marriage for Aderonke. How can she get over Remi with these suitors around all the time? She cannot leave her own house. She cannot busy herself with anything. She cannot visit anyone...."

"That's it!" Bimpe decisively slapped her hand on the mat. "Don't you see, Eli? That's it!"

"Whatever do you mean, Bimpe?"

"Aderonke can go visit someone far from here for a while, and the suitors will give up. They will make marriages somewhere else and leave off harassing you and your family. And perhaps the police will have found those thugs and be able to find out which of the suitors was behind Remi's disappearance. When that police officer no longer spends his time making constant rounds to your house, he might get busy finding the murderers!"

"Oh, Bimpe, do you think we could do it?" Eli's face lit up for a moment, but it was soon clouded with worry again. "No...no, it wouldn't work. I really fear violence. If one of those suitors has done away with Remi, how might he react if we were to try to send Aderonke away? He might attack her on the road, or he might attack us in anger when he finds out she is gone. He might even seek her out wherever we send her, and we would not be there to protect her! What if," she whispered, "the murderer is the police officer? He could do any amount of harm and cover it up so that no one would ever know!"

Bimpe nodded and said, "You're right, but there must be a way. The situation cannot go on like this, and it will only get worse with time. We must do something to get Aderonke out of here and gain some peace for you and your husband. I'm sure this is not doing his heart any good."

"No," Eli said, looking more worried than ever. "I'm afraid we have all been worn down. And Aderonke is our only child. What would we do if anything terrible happened to her? She is already pining away, and that has me worried enough."

Both women stared at the mat, following the weave with their eyes, not really seeing it at all. They were both deep in thought.

Then something strange happened; just as Bimpe raised her eyes, Eli did the same. Just as a smile began to crease Eli's worried face, a smile began to form on Bimpe's. And just as one began to speak, so did the other.

"She's pining away!" they said in unison.

Aderonke's grandfather came to visit that very afternoon. This was most unusual. Aderonke's grandfather was the medicine man of a tiny village nearby. He was a very important person, and he did not go to visit people—they went to visit him. When he walked up to Aderonke's house, all the young men standing around backed off to leave him plenty of room. The black dog came out and danced around his legs, wagging his tail. Eli met Aderonke's grandfather at the door.

The word spread quickly throughout the town. When Aderonke's grandfather left two hours later, the crowd outside had grown quite a bit larger, although each suitor tried to look as if he had some business nearby.

Aderonke's grandfather looked grimmer than usual. He spoke to no one, and he was soon out of sight as he walked briskly down the path to his own village.

Bimpe came to visit again the next day, and this time she and Eli went out for a midafternoon walk. As they came out of the house to go on their walk, neither woman looked at any of the suitors. Eli held her head down, shaking it slowly and looking terribly sad. Bimpe supported her as she walked.

They walked along a path at the edge of town to a brook located there. For a while they sat on a large rock by the brook, and every once in a while Bimpe would put her arm around Eli and pat her on the shoulder.

They returned after about an hour. Bimpe again physically supported her friend as Eli stumbled along, seeming not to see where she was going. The suitors standing around Aderonke's house were so surprised by this unusual behavior that they let the women pass without a word.

Bimpe spent the night at Aderonke's house, and when she left the next morning, she looked twenty years older than she had the day before. Two young men who had already managed to find an excuse to be near Aderonke's house looked at each other with puzzled expressions on their faces, but they did not bother Bimpe as she walked slowly home.

That afternoon Bimpe returned. She looked better than she had in the morning, but she entered the house without a word and did not come out again.

When the police officer came by "to report on the progress of the investigation," Aderonke's father met him at the door. He, too, appeared much older than his actual age, and the police officer was taken aback. *What could be wrong? Has the old man run out of his medication?* He wondered.

"Good evening, sir," he said politely. "I hope you are well."

"Good evening," Aderonke's father said with a sigh. "I am afraid I am not as well as I might be, but do come in and tell me what you have discovered." Aderonke's father managed a small but brave smile.

"Uh...yes," the police officer said, looking around to see where Aderonke might be. "Well, I have several men following up leads in some nearby towns. And there is one report that the men were seen in the capital, although I fail to see how they could have gotten so far."

"Perhaps they had plenty of money," Aderonke's father suggested. He sighed once more.

"Um...yes, perhaps. I would not like to say exactly what our suspicions are with regard to who hired them—you understand, I'm sure."

"Oh, yes, I understand," Aderonke's father said. "I understand perfectly." He let his eyes wander to the floor, and there his gaze remained. His shoulders sagged, and he sighed again.

"Sir?" the police officer asked as deferentially as possible. "May I help you in some way? Are you ill?" The police officer tried his best to look helpful and unofficial, which was particularly difficult for him because he spent most of his time trying to look businesslike and even downright threatening.

Aderonke's father looked startled by the police officer's questions. He said, "Oh, I am sorry. Please forgive my rudeness. It's Aderonke, you know."

"Aderonke? I don't understand, sir."

The police officer shifted uneasily. He knew that now that there was an investigation going on, the other suitors would be nervous about visiting Aderonke if he were around; after all, he might implicate any one of them in Remi's disappearance and probable murder. If he could just come around often enough and drag the investigation out long enough, Aderonke would be his. He hoped there was no difficulty that might stand in his way now that victory was within his grasp.

Aderonke's father sighed again, more deeply than ever. In a very low voice, he finally said, "She is very ill."

"Ill!" the police officer shouted in surprise. Aderonke was a remarkably healthy and vibrant young lady. He had never thought of her as being ill. Surely he could not lose her now!

"Yes," her father said. "You see, she seems to have taken after me. With her heart, that is. These very upsetting events of the past few days have broken her spirit. I don't suppose you know..."—although Aderonke's father knew perfectly well that the police officer did indeed know—"but her grandfather came by two days ago. He has worked his strongest medicine for her, and I have even given her some of the medication from the pharmacist's shop. But all to no avail. She is sinking moment by moment, and I fear we shall be childless within the week." Aderonke's father put upon his face the bravest and most manly look, setting his jaw firmly against his sorrow.

The poor police officer was genuinely shocked. He was, in fact, a rather spoiled young man who had gotten everything he really wanted all his life, and right now he really wanted Aderonke. But more than that, he truly fancied himself in love with her, and he was heartbroken at the idea that she might be dying. If only he had been more aggressive in his courting! If only he had already caught the murderers! If only he had known sooner that Aderonke was ill!

He wanted to do several things at once—marry Aderonke, catch the criminals, somehow make Aderonke well again—but he did not know how to do any of these things. For someone who was used to getting his way all his life, it was hard to come up against such a frustration. The police officer paced around the room, banging one fist into the other hand over and over. Finally, he stopped and looked at Aderonke's father, who had not risen from his place on the mat nor straightened his slumping shoulders.

"May I see her, sir?" he pleaded. "If she should die, I want her to know how much I wanted her for my wife. And if she should not die, I want her to know how much I care about her. I would do anything at all to make her well again!"

"Just a moment," Aderonke's father said. "I will see if she is awake." He left the room, and it seemed to the police officer as if he were gone for over an hour before he came back.

"Well," he reported, "I think you may come in for just a moment. My dear wife believes the child cannot last much longer, and it will make little difference. The room is dark, you understand, because the light seems to hurt Aderonke's eyes."

The police officer stumbled after Aderonke's father to the door of the young woman's room. It certainly was dark. Eli and Bimpe sat beside Aderonke's bed, fanning Aderonke constantly and wiping her forehead with cool water. Aderonke herself was completely bundled up. Her face looked ashen, and her eyes were closed.

"Aderonke?" the police officer whispered. "Aderonke, I have come to see you."

Aderonke's eyelids fluttered slightly and then opened slowly. This small movement seemed to require tremendous effort. She could not seem to focus, however, and her eyelids shut again. Her lips hardly moved as Aderonke spoke in the barest of broken whispers, so the police officer bent down to hear her more clearly.

"I am glad you came. I am so sorry....I'm tired."

"Oh, you must rest, dear Aderonke," the police officer said. He looked at the two older women, swallowed nervously, and continued, "I wanted you to know how very much I want you for my wife. Please get well, dear Aderonke, and I will do anything at all to win you!"

Aderonke smiled the tiniest of smiles, but she did not speak again.

After a few moments, the police officer rose, said good-bye to Aderonke's father, and strode out of the house looking remarkably official, businesslike, and threatening. The other suitors kept well out of his way.

It was early evening when the police officer returned. This time he brought his father with him. The police officer's father and Aderonke's father had been friends long ago in their schooldays, though they had not had much contact since Aderonke's family returned from the city. Nevertheless, there was still much warmth between them.

"Ah, my dear friend," the police officer's father said, "I am so very sorry to hear of your daughter's illness. I have come to see if I may be of some help."

Aderonke's father replied, "I thank you for coming, my friend. As your son has no doubt told you, we have done everything we could think of doing. Yet she seems to sink further each day."

"Have you thought of the district hospital?" the police officer's father asked.

"The hospital? No...no, I haven't. I do not know what they could do for her there that we have not done already. And no one in our family has ever been in the hospital before, so I am sure Aderonke would be terribly frightened."

"Oh, no! Surely not!" the police officer's father said. "She would be cared for by nurses close to her own age, young women she would feel at ease with. I have been there myself, and it is altogether a pleasant place."

"Perhaps you are right," Aderonke's father said. "But would it not be dangerous to move her, being so ill? Even though I am certain she cannot live much longer as she is, I would not want to hasten her end."

"We could move her with a police helicopter," the police officer suggested. "I could get one from district headquarters this very night!"

Aderonke's father thought carefully for a few minutes. If Aderonke were taken to the district hospital in the police helicopter, she would not be here in town. The sooner she was out of town, the better—yes, this would fit in nicely with his plans.

"That sounds like a good idea," he finally said. "How soon should I have Aderonke ready?"

Aderonke was taken to the hospital that night. The police officer called for a helicopter, which landed close to Aderonke's house. All bundled up, Aderonke was placed on a stretcher and then carefully put aboard. Her father accompanied her, but her mother stayed home, and Bimpe stayed with Eli to comfort her. The police officer, feeling very important, saw the helicopter off and told the gawking bystanders to disperse if they knew what was good for them.

Everyone in town was saddened four days later when Aderonke's father returned with the news that poor Aderonke had died soon after reaching the hospital.

Her parents, who had kept careful track of the many gifts Aderonke had received from her suitors, returned them all. This took quite a long time, as on each occasion there were many expressions of condolences and regret on the part of the suitor and many brave smiles and expressions of gratitude on the part of Aderonke's parents. After a time, however, the suitors began to acquire new lady friends, and Aderonke's parents settled down to a quiet, peaceful life.

# FIVE

Remi choked, and then he cried out in pain. His chest and belly felt as if they had been burned—and they were still burning. He rolled over gingerly, squinting his eyes against the sun.

He looked down at his chest. There was a long gash, and sand had just gotten into it when he rather suddenly washed up on shore. *No, this is not the shore*, Remi reflected. *What is this? Where am I?*

Remi pulled himself painfully up to a sitting position and looked around. He was on a narrow strip of sand and sharp white rock, with the billowing sea on one side and what appeared to be a shallow lake on the other. As his eyes adjusted to the bright sun, however, he could see that the lake actually ended in gentle breakers lapping against a wide beach some distance away. A rain forest sat behind the beach. The little strip of sand on which he sat continued generally parallel to the beach. It was broken in a few places, allowing the sea free access, and it occasionally widened out and was overgrown with grasses in some spots.

Remi had washed up on a coral reef, although he did not know that, as he had never been more than two days' walking distance from his home until now. He could see that the water on one side of his little sand strip had every appearance of ordinary ocean—something he had seen far too much of for far too long—and he also noticed that the water on the other side was remarkably calm and clear so that he could just make out the bottom.

Remi winced as he tried to get a better view. The gash was not the only injury he had sustained. He realized that he was bruised from head to foot, and there were many small cuts all over his body. He felt stiff, miserable, and tired.

And thirsty. Remi's tongue was swollen, his lips were cracked, and his throat was nearly closed. If he did not get to shore soon, he would die here on the reef.

Remi dragged himself to the inner side of the reef and splashed his face with water. He would have to make one more effort, and soon he would be on land. There would be fresh water and food. Perhaps there would be people who could help him get back home to Aderonke.

With the thought of Aderonke, Remi gained the energy to plunge back into the water and swim toward the beach. He was fortunate to be on the incoming tide; he was so weak that he would not have made it otherwise. Even so, when he came to the beach, he found that he did not have the strength to get out of the water. He sat on the wet sand, letting the little breakers swirl and eddy around him. The water had risen almost to his shoulders before he finally summoned up the strength to get to his feet.

Remi knew that drinking water was the most important priority now, and he felt that were he to sit down again before he found it, he might never get back up. He crossed the hot white sand and walked along the edge of the thick vegetation. Here he was at least in partial shade, and he could see if there were any rivulets coming down to the beach.

He could not walk very fast—in fact, he actually staggered rather than walked. Every once in a while, he stopped and listened, but he did not have the strength to call out to anyone had he heard another human being. Not that it mattered; Remi heard no voices at any time and saw no sign whatsoever of any other people.

Remi had walked for some time when he finally came upon a tiny stream trickling through the grass. He followed it down to where it met the sand and found a small pool. He cupped the water in his hands and drank eagerly. He could barely swallow at first, and it was a long time before he had begun to slake his thirst.

Then he lay in the grass and slept.

Remi was not sure how long he had slept, but when he awoke, the stars appeared to be just leaving the sky. Soon there was a reddening on the horizon, and then the sun rose. At least now he knew which way was east—and that told him that he had not washed up on any land near his own country, for he lived on the extreme western coast. There was only ocean to the east.

Remi's heart sank as he pondered his situation. *Could I have been swept all the way to South America? No, that is impossible! It would have taken many more days, and I would be quite dead. Then I must be on an island, but I have never heard of any island, especially any island with people on it, between my own coast and that of South America. I am utterly lost!*

He felt stiffer than ever, having lain still for so long, and he was hungrier than he had ever been in his entire life. Happily, the wounds on his chest and belly seemed to be healing. (He must have cut himself badly on the coral reef when he washed up on it.) After slowly inspecting himself, he came to the conclusion that aside from being terribly bruised and having some annoying cuts, he was probably in good condition.

He was thirsty again, of course. He would need to drink a lot of water for the next few days. . . .

. . . And then it seemed to hit him for the first time. He was marooned on some little island that was probably uninhabited. He could not swim across the ocean, and no ships were likely to pass that way. A raft would likely wash right back onto the coral reef because of the current and because he had absolutely no skills in seamanship. Remi was a farmer, and even though his little town served as a minor port, he had been out in a dinghy only once: when the thugs tried to do away with him and nearly succeeded. He could not get home. He could not get to Aderonke.

Despite his puffy tongue, parched lips, and raw throat, Remi yelled. It was an angry yell like that of some animal mother who had lost her children. It was a yell of despair and fury. He pounded his feet into the sand in a furious dance such as he had never danced back home, and whenever his yelling took on the form of any word at all, that word was "Aderonke!"

Remi exhausted himself with his dance and his wordless song and his anger and despair. Eventually, he collapsed on the sand, and it was a long time before he stirred.

Remi then set about looking for food. Occasionally, the thought crossed his mind that there was no reason for him to eat—what did he have to live for now that he would never see Aderonke again? But some other part of him seemed to reach for life in spite of himself.

When he started looking for something to eat, Remi discovered that he had landed in a place overflowing with food. Only a hundred paces from the beach, he found several different kinds of trees bearing fruits he had never seen before—along with his own familiar pawpaw. He found other large fruits growing on vines along the ground, and he was glad to find yams as well. He ventured into the sea again, exploring the shallow water this side of the reef, and he was astonished at what he found.

The strange white stone that had cut him so badly seemed to grow in great lumps and ridges under the water, and among them swam more kinds of fish than Remi had ever imagined. They were unlike any other fish he had seen, all of them brightly colored and outlandishly patterned. The fish did not seem particularly worried about his presence, and Remi found that he could actually catch one in his hands.

Firewood was no problem at all. There were clumps of driftwood here and there on the beach and plenty of timber at the edges of the forest. With a pang in his heart, Remi thought of his mother gathering wood for sale back in the village and wondered if she and his sister thought him dead.

Starting a fire presented some difficulty. Remi had always used a flint for this purpose, although as a boy he had learned to get the flames going with a couple sticks. It took him the better part of an hour to perfect his technique and encourage a small blaze.

Remi quieted his immediate hunger with some pawpaw and then gathered a huge stack of firewood. He decided it would be best to keep a fire going all the time if he possibly could, as there was plenty of wood and it was so hard to start a fire without a flint. Then, too, a fire would ward off any large animals and possibly attract the notice of some passing ship.

Because he had to stop and rest every few minutes, this task took most of the afternoon. The sun fell behind the trees before he was able to sit down and enjoy baked fish and roasted yams. He tried a tiny amount of an unfamiliar fruit. If it was poisonous, he would probably simply get sick instead of dying from it. If it was good to eat, there was plenty more where that came from. And there would be plenty of tomorrows in which to experiment with his diet....

At that thought, Remi gritted his teeth. Plenty of tomorrows without Aderonke. What could he do?

He banked the fire up for the night and lay down beside it, gazing up at the stars. His mind was clearer now that he had eaten—and now that his first outburst of rage and despair was spent. Could he get off the island and back to his home?

Probably not. A raft would not do, and he had no knowledge of how to build or use a boat. There were plenty of trees—could any of them be large enough and easy enough for him to cut to make a dugout canoe? Could he find any material from which to make a sail?

His own clothing now solely consisted of a ragged pair of shorts of the kind worn by everyone in his village. His shirt had either been removed by the thugs after they bopped him over the head or been taken by the ocean; he could not remember. He knew nothing about how to weave cloth, assuming that he could find any plant that would produce a fiber suitable for weaving. Thus, a sail of any sort was highly unlikely. But he would keep it in mind. It would certainly not hurt to look for fiber-bearing plants or for a tree that might make an ocean-going canoe.

What about getting the attention of passing ships? The fire would be quite useful there. Maybe he shouldn't bank it at night, but build it up to a great blaze instead? And in the daytime, he should try to make it smoke as much as possible, using damp wood or even leaves.

Could he build anything else that might attract attention? A tower? Some sort of structure out on the narrow sandspit where the reef began? That would certainly be noticeable to passing ships, but whatever he built was likely to be knocked down in any kind of storm. Getting wood out there would be difficult, and wood would disappear faster than stone. Could he take stone out to the reef?

Perhaps he should build a small raft. He might find that handy for a variety of purposes, even though it would do him no good in getting off the island. Yes, he would start work on a small raft tomorrow.

But what about shelter? Could he live on the beach indefinitely? Right now the weather was perfect: no rain, clear skies, and not nearly as hot as he would have expected. Was this likely to last? Remi didn't know, but he did know that he wouldn't enjoy being exposed to several weeks of driving rain or unbearable heat. He decided to devise some sort of shelter first.

Remi considered his options. He could build a regular house of wood, but the effort and time involved in building even the crudest house would be considerable because he had no tools to work with. He thought back to his town and remembered that the buildings along the shore were built on piles. Perhaps that construction offered protection against storms and the raging of the sea. Without tools, he figured he should probably not try something so elaborate. Perhaps next year, if he was still here....

Angrily, he gritted his teeth. *There is no point in getting upset,* he thought. *I could be here for the rest of my life. It makes sense to plan ahead just in case. But meanwhile, I should find some easier method of constructing shelter.*

It probably should be well past the beach, under the trees—but not too far, so he could have a clear view up and down the beach and out to sea. Remi had no idea whether there were any large and dangerous animals on the island, but he had to take that possibility into consideration. Perhaps a tree house would be the best shelter. It would offer some protection against intruders, and a really suitable tree would provide some of the basic structure for him.

Food and water seemed to present no significant problems. From what he had seen, this island grew plenty of food for one person and would continue to grow it without any assistance from him. Tomorrow he would look for a larger source of freshwater, but he was sure plenty was available because the vegetation was so lush.

Remi wondered fleetingly what he would wear after his shorts wore out completely, which wouldn't be long. But by this time, he was very weary....His next thought was his surprise at having slept well past sunrise.

Remi breakfasted hastily on some of the unknown fruit, which seemed not to have done him any damage and was both sweet and very full of refreshing juice. He built the fire up and then put plenty of wet wood on it so that it would smoke. He drew a large arrow in the sand, pointing in the direction he intended to go.

He followed the rivulet some distance into the forest and discovered that it originated in a little spring. With his hands, he dug in the soft, sandy mud around the spring and formed a small pool. While he was waiting for the water to settle, he looked carefully for a tree that might serve as a base for his tree house.

One was close by. It was quite large around the trunk and branching off to one side so that it looked downright lopsided. It featured a low fork with some side branches; with a little work, it would provide a sturdy floor for Remi's new home. There were plenty of heavy vines, or lianas, climbing the larger trees, and although there were few tiny trees in the forest, several were at its edge near the beach. Remi had ample material for his building, but he still had no tools.

He went back to check on the spring, which was filling the little pool nicely. Then he walked back to the beach, deep in thought. *What could I use for tools?*

While considering this matter, Remi wandered about and picked up stones to line his little pool so that it would not fill up with mud again. None of the stones was sharp enough to use for a tool, and he wasn't sure they would be the right kind anyway. How he wished for his own machete!

Suddenly, Remi noticed something among the stones. It was a large shell, almost a foot across. It was also curved and had a little lip on it that would fit the hand nicely. The edge opposite the lip was broken, jagged, and quite sharp. The shell was also heavy enough that it might possibly serve as a sort of rudimentary machete.

Remi tried to cut a small branch off one of the young trees near the beach. It was awkward, but it worked. A combination of dogged hacking and determined sawing brought the limb off the tree and into Remi's hand in a short time.

The rest of that day was taken up entirely with more hacking and sawing. The limbs came off fairly easily after Remi developed a technique, but he had far more trouble severing enough of the lianas to bind his branches together. He was glad they were tough—after all, he wanted them to hold his house in one piece—but doubly sorry he did not have proper tools.

Remi ate a large supper that evening, and when he lay down to sleep, he had no time at all for planning out the next day.

When Remi awoke the next morning, his muscles were stiff and sore in new places, but he went right back to work. He laid the floor of the tree house and fashioned a sturdy ladder for easy access. After the floor was in place, the rest of the building went up swiftly, and Remi was pleasantly surprised when he realized he could spend the night in his new home. He created a roof of braided grass and topped it with broad leaves that would repel any rain, though there hadn't been a cloud in the sky since he landed on the island. By sundown, he had ensconced himself in his tree house for the night.

Remi spent his fifth day on the island further exploring his surroundings. Using the shell as a machete gave him ideas about possible uses for other kinds of shells, and he wanted to swim through the reef to find some.

Remi's underwater investigations proved interesting. He brought several different kinds of shells to the beach and pried out their inhabitants, which provided an excellent dinner for him that evening. Some of the shells had fine holes in them, some had larger ones, and some had none at all. Some were so shaped that they would make decent cups, buckets, and other containers. One was just right to serve as a pot for stew. A few had sharp edges and seemed ready-made for use as tools.

Remi fashioned himself a short spear for use underwater. *This will be easier than catching fish in my hands,* he thought. He was also able to make a sling, with which he hoped to catch some of the plump birds he had occasionally seen on the beach. Then he built up his fire with wet wood and made an arrow in the sand, this time pointing down the beach to the south.

As he walked, Remi counted off his paces. Every time he reached a hundred, he made a long mark across the beach. Coming back, he would count the marks to see how far he had gone. He wanted to get some idea as to how large his island kingdom was.

Remi walked about half the afternoon. He found two more places where rivulets worked their way through the vegetation and down to the sea. One of them really should have been called a creek because by the time it crossed the beach, it was wider than the span of his arms but not a handspan deep. By the time the sun was low enough in the sky that he knew he should turn back, the beach had turned and was running due west. He strained his eyes as far west as he could see, but there was nothing other than the thin line of beach and a great deal of blue water, with the little line of reef off to his left.

On his way back, Remi noticed several piles of driftwood, and he also realized that the forest at one place receded from the beach for several hundred paces. Here hundreds of birds stood in the grass, and the grass was so near the level of the sea that it was marshy and wet. He tried out his sling, but his efforts were to no avail; there was something wrong with the design, and he couldn't get enough power behind his pebbles.

Remi stopped at the creek, gauged the time by the sun, and decided he still had time to find out more about the creek's source. He was pleasantly surprised when he discovered that the creek turned north not far inside the forest. With any luck, its source might be near his present home.

When he returned to his fire, Remi found that he had walked about six miles before turning back. Looking to the north, he could see plainly that the island must run from east to west; the north-south distance was only a mile at most. Tomorrow he would explore in the other direction.

The next day, Remi went north. He found quite a bit more driftwood—much more than he had found to the south—and five more rivulets (but no creek). It was only about half a mile before the shore turned to the west, and then it actually turned southwest as far as the eye could see. Apparently, the island was almost triangular.

Because he had allotted the entire day for walking, to see if he could come completely around to where he had stopped the day before, Remi walked many miles that day. He did not quite come to the far western tip of the island, but he came close enough to be just about certain where it was and how big the island was. He figured that it was about a mile on the north-south side, eight miles on the east-west side, and nine or ten miles on the long side.

He saw a great many birds again, though he did not find another marsh. He saw no sign that any human being had ever been there, however, and he saw no four-legged animals at all.

On the seventh day, Remi decided to look for the source of the creek. On an island this size, this creek was probably the largest "river," and it would be well worth exploring.

He walked part of the way south and cut across the beach and into the forest. Sure enough, within five hundred paces, he had located the creek, and it was still coming from the north. He followed it upstream for a time, but then it turned west. It was still early in the day, and Remi decided to follow it for a while longer.

Remi was surprised to find the land rising slightly as he walked along. He had thought the island was nearly flat. He was even more surprised when he came out into sunlight from under the trees. Low bushes surrounded the creek and the pool from which it was running. Above the pool was a ledge of black stone, and the water was coming over the ledge and into the pool.

All the stones around the pool were black, such as Remi had never seen before. This made it difficult to tell how deep the pool was, so Remi lowered himself into it to find out.

He could not touch bottom without going down so deep that he couldn't see at all, but the water in the pool was clear and refreshing. This was the first time Remi had had freshwater all over his body, and it felt like the best medicine for his physical aches and pains. He was reluctant to climb out.

Remi sat on a black stone to let the sun dry him off. What a beautiful place on such a forsaken island! It was so peaceful here, so refreshing....He let his thoughts drift, and they naturally drifted to Aderonke.

It was sometime before Remi stood up and started back to his new home. A plan was beginning to form in his mind.

On his eighth day on the island, Remi set about implementing his plan. It would take a long time—but then again, he had all the time in the world.

It took him several days to fashion some of the things he would need: a finely woven basket, a larger sort of bag, a sturdy pry bar, a raft, and a long pole that he judged would reach to the bottom of the deepest part of the sea between the beach and the barrier reef. He took special care in making each of these—and other—items because they were to be used for a very special purpose, a sacred purpose.

Remi found great joy in his work.

After Remi had prepared his tools, he set about the next part of the task. Every day he went swimming in the shallow waters of the reef, but he spent little time looking for dinner. Instead, he ranged far both north and south, occasionally removing some shell or rock or particularly beautiful piece of coral and putting it in his bag. When the shell was inhabited, dinner took care of itself—but Remi was really more interested in the shell.

Each day after swimming, Remi walked back home up the beach, occasionally picking up some shell or rock or curiously shaped piece of driftwood and putting it in his bag. When he came to the rivulet near home, Remi carefully washed the sand out of the items he had gathered and laid them out on the grass to dry.

As his collection began to grow, Remi decided he needed several more baskets. He spent nearly a week working out a special design for these baskets, and then he spent many more days making the baskets themselves. When he had finished them, he sorted out his collection and arranged the items in the baskets with the utmost care. He then placed each basket along the wall of the tree house opposite the entrance.

Looking at this arrangement, Remi decided it appeared a little bare. He spent one whole afternoon gathering flowers, especially some of the large red blooms that grew near the waterfall, and fastening them to the wall above the baskets.

From then on, after each day's swimming, Remi brought his new collection to the tree house and incorporated the items into the arrangements in the baskets. Every few days, he took an afternoon off to gather flowers and renew them on the wall above the baskets; he reverently cast the old blossoms out to sea.

When the entire wall of the tree house was decorated with a row of full baskets, Remi turned his attention elsewhere. He began to take the raft out each day, poling his way up and down the reef. Every once in a while, he pulled over to the beach to grab a rather sizable rock, which he placed on the raft. One time he decided to go all the way around the island in case he should miss any particularly suitable rocks by not going far enough. This took him several days because his was a painstakingly careful search.

From the far western point of the island, Remi could see a forested hill on the island. He supposed this must be the hill where the waterfall was located, but he had not realized that it went up much farther than the top of the waterfall. Except for the marsh on the south side of the island, there seemed to be only rain forest and beach.

Remi came back from this lengthy trip with about thirty rocks—a heavy load for his little raft and tough going for him to pole through the reef. Again, he carefully washed the sand from each rock and set them out to dry. But he did not take the rocks to the tree house.

Altogether Remi had gathered nearly a hundred rocks. He now began to load them onto the raft and carry them out to the barrier. When he got them there, he sorted them out according to size and shape, and he began to build.

Remi first had to dig down slightly into the sand. He hoped to anchor his rocks firmly in the branches of coral that undergirded the sand, and after a few tries in different places, he found what looked like a solid grounding for his structure. Then he selected six of the largest rocks and spent a great deal of time laying them for a foundation. With the exception of a gap in the very middle, he fit them together so that there were no spaces in between the stones.

Then Remi rummaged around in a basket on his raft and brought out three objects. One was a rather small but perfect white blossom of a flower that bloomed every morning but wilted at night. The second was a shell that reflected every color in the rainbow on the inside and was perfectly shaped on the outside as if a sculptor had made it. Finally, a statue of Aderonke that Remi had laboriously carved from a piece of driftwood, using a sharp shell.

Remi placed the blossom inside the shell, and he laid the tiny wooden figure inside the blossom. He reverently placed these items in the center of his six stones.

"There," he said aloud, "how do you like that, Aderonke? What do you think? Will that be comfortable?

I want you to be as comfortable as possible. Now you must help me with the rest of this building."

Remi worked all afternoon. He tried first one stone, then another. He built a stone column, or cairn, that was slightly smaller at the top than at the bottom. He strove to make the fit as perfect as he could so that the cairn would be solid.

All the stones were quite large, but he had selected them carefully so that they would have fairly straight sides and fit together well. When he was finished, the cairn came up to Remi's heart.

Now Remi set about the second stage of his building.

Without a decent machete, he had a hard time clearing a path to the little waterfall—it was much easier to walk up the little creek bed. But clear a path he did. He first widened the path from the beach to his own house, then he cut through the forest to the north side of the creek, and finally he ran the path alongside the creek to the waterfall and the pool.

This took a great deal of time and effort. Remi was happy to learn that the forest floor was not particularly overgrown with small, quick-growing plants—mostly it was composed of various kinds of shrubs and broad-leafed plants with bright flowers, and it was fairly easy to cut a path through these and not have them grow back over his path within a week. Cutting a path along the creek was a bit more difficult because the plants there tended to grow up again practically as soon as they were cut. Nevertheless, Remi kept at his task, and he found that constant use of the path kept it open with minimal extra cutting.

He walked the whole distance to the waterfall every day and took a quick swim in the pool, but he made no attempt to find the bottom or to climb past the waterfall to the top of the hill.

When he was about two-thirds of the way through with cutting his path, the rains came.

For weeks, rain poured both day and night. Sometimes it let up to a mere drizzle, but in the space of over a month, Remi could not remember as much as an hour when there was no rain at all. He spent most of his time in the tree house, which did offer him shelter, though with that much rain, there was no way he could actually stay dry. Quite a bit of Remi's time was spent trying to keep his collection of shells and other beautiful objects from getting wet. He was pleased that despite the heavy rain, there was little wind, so at least he did not have to battle a swaying, shifting tree house.

The sea also stayed relatively calm. Remi had imagined that if it rained, the sea would be in a terrible uproar. The waves were somewhat higher than usual, and they did break over the barrier occasionally, but Remi's monument on the barrier did not fall.

Despite the rain and the more difficult surf, Remi took his raft or swam to the barrier each day. There he checked the condition of the cairn and talked to his statue of Aderonke.

He sat on the barrier sand beside the monument, looking out to sea. The rain had stopped for a few hours now, and the sun had come out for the first time in several weeks. Remi felt as if his skin had been pickled, and he was glad to feel the sun's warmth.

"What shall I do now, Aderonke?" Remi asked. "I'll finish the path in the next few days if the rain holds off, and I suppose I should make a good search of the beach to see if any beautiful things washed up during all this rain. Then I need to get everything in place...and, Aderonke, then you will see my real surprise! All this is just the beginning!" Remi patted the cairn fondly and said, "Tomorrow I will bring you flowers."

He remembered his promise. Almost all the next day was spent clearing the path, but he went out to the cairn in the late afternoon. On his raft, he carried a large basket of the big red blossoms, and he made these into a garland. As he draped the garland around the monument, he spoke aloud of his progress.

"Well, Aderonke, I hope you like these. I've been working on the path all day, and I'm thinking I need to make some improvements there. I don't know how often it rains like this—maybe only once a year, but then again, things may get worse. There might be some stronger storms, and that path is muddy. I'm thinking of putting down something to keep the mud out. What do you think?"

Remi contemplated the cairn for a time and then spoke again, "I don't know about sand. I think it might wash away. Gravel would be better, but I don't know of any around here. The beach is all such fine sand that it's almost powdery, and finding big rocks isn't easy." He paused and gazed at the cairn thoughtfully. "I'd need lots rocks about this size, and they'd have to be flat on one side. That path's about half a mile long, I'll bet. That'd require an incredible amount of rock!"

Remi sat down and leaned against the stones.

"Why, of course! Thank you, Aderonke! I knew you could help me figure it out. I'll just find and lay one stone each day. It will take years to finish, but I have years to work on it. And what a fine shrine it will make when I am through! If anyone ever comes this way, he will find such a monument to you that it will make him honor such a fine lady, Aderonke!"

Remi jumped up and patted the cairn affectionately. Before sunset, he found and laid the first stone on the path to the waterfall.

Remi finished clearing the path ten days later, and there was no more rain for the time being. Every day he added a new stone to the beginning of the path through the forest, and every day he took more flowers out to the cairn and discussed his plans with Aderonke. But he kept part of his plan entirely to himself.

If Aderonke had been listening, she would have heard Remi singing in the tree house at night.

Now that the path was cleared, Remi carried his baskets of beautiful shells and other objects up to the waterfall. There was a sort of rock shelf underneath the overhang; part of this was deep enough to sit on.

Remi floated his baskets across the pool and under the waterfall to the rock shelf and pulled himself up out of the water. Then he spent nearly a full day arranging and rearranging the objects on the rock shelf, but the space in the middle he left open for later use. As he worked, he spoke aloud.

"You see, Aderonke? This shell is shaped like your eyes. How could I ever forget such a beautiful shape? Does not every man want something beautiful? If you will not come to be with me, I will come to be with you whenever I look at this shell and think of your eyes....Look at me with your beautiful eyes, Aderonke!"

Remi took a small piece of driftwood from a basket and asked, "Do you know who this is, Aderonke? It's that terrible, fierce dog of yours. I guess I have him tamed now! But he will let only me pass into your home, only me! No more hundreds of suitors! No more police officer and pharmacist and farmer and palm-wine seller and sailor! This is our secret place together, Aderonke. Let him scare everyone else away, so I can have you all to myself!"

Remi smiled as he placed the driftwood dog on one end of the shelf.

"Look at this! It took me a long time to gather enough of these all the same color and size. Aren't they pretty? They remind me of your teeth—only your teeth aren't pink! Like jewels, perhaps....You know that I could never afford to give you jewels or other fancy gifts, but these are prettier than any jewels I've ever seen."

Each item was carefully described for Aderonke and put in its proper place. It was nearly sunset when Remi made his way back down the path with the empty baskets.

Remi was now ready to undertake the most important part of his preparations.

One of the trees near his own tree house (and many more throughout the forest) had an unusual kind of bark. Remi noticed that the bark seemed very thin and that it could be peeled off the trees in strips. He experimented carefully, not willing to damage any of the trees but wanting to find out whether this bark could serve his intended purpose. Over many days, he stripped different-sized pieces of bark from several of these trees and brought them to the tree house.

The bark was soft on the inside, a kind of reddish-brown color, and smooth to the touch. Remi found that if he marked on this side of the bark with a sharp stick, the color came away, and his markings remained in a yellowish-gray. He also discovered that as the bark dried, it curled up and could not be unwound again without breaking it. He tried rubbing it with the sap of the tree to keep it pliable, but this strategy did not work very well.

He carried the bark out to the beach and tried rubbing it with various combinations of seawater and sap, then weighing it down with stones to let it dry in the sun. That didn't work either; the bark cracked in the sun.

He tried wrapping the bark in leaves smeared with the sap and letting it dry slowly on the grass.

This worked much better, leaving the bark supple enough that he could roll it up and then unroll it again.

Remi tried this method on several strips before he got one that satisfied him. It was as long as the span of his arms and about two handspans wide. He worked a long time on trimming the edges with a sharp shell, and he dyed the outside of the bark with the juice of some purple berries.

Using the bark, he cut and sharpened several sticks. As he worked on each of these, he occasionally sang a little song:

> We will bring Aderonke near to us.
> We will bring Aderonke near to us.
> We will bring Aderonke to our tree house!
> Aderonke will come to our tree house!
> Aderonke will come to our island!
>
> We will bring Aderonke near to us.
> We will bring Aderonke near to us.
> We will bring Aderonke to our waterfall!
> Aderonke will come to our waterfall!
> Aderonke will come to our island!
>
> We will bring Aderonke near to us.
> We will bring Aderonke near to us.

*We will bring Aderonke to our forest home!*
*Aderonke will come to our forest home!*
*Aderonke will come to our island!*

It took Remi a very long time to make these little sticks. Several times, when he was almost finished creating one, he looked at it critically and discarded it only to start crafting a new one.

Finally, Remi had six sticks, each identical to the other and each very sharp. He was quite pleased with himself, and that evening he swam out to the cairn with an especially jolly wreath of yellow and orange blossoms. But he did not talk to Aderonke about what he had been doing.

That night he could be heard singing in the tree house for a long time.

The next day, Remi proclaimed a festival. It would begin at the full moon and last until the dark of the moon, and it would be held in Aderonke's honor.

There were still several days of preparation left. Remi went swimming with his spear and caught several large fish. He built a deep firepit and collected a massive quantity of firewood. He gathered berries and yams and all kinds of fruits. He took his new, improved sling and went to the marsh, and when he came back, his bag was full of multicolored birds.

Remi fashioned a beautiful cloak of feathers—pink, white, red, and gray—and several gorgeous necklaces of iridescent shells. He made a dazzling crown of feathers and shells, too. These he set aside in the tree house while he made a second cloak, somewhat longer than the first, and many other ornaments of shells and feathers. The tree house sprouted feathers and flowers all around the door and down the ladder.

And on the day of the full moon, Remi rafted out to the barrier. He wore the larger feather cloak, and his arms, neck, and legs were bravely decked out in vibrant ornaments.

When Remi grounded the raft, he carefully removed the smaller feather cloak from a basket and placed it around the "shoulders" of the cairn. He draped several shell necklaces over the cloak and put the shell-and-feather crown on the top.

"There, Aderonke!" he exclaimed. "You are all dressed up for the festival in your honor. Welcome to our island!"

For the next several days, Remi feasted in honor of Aderonke. Every day he carried more flowers to her monument, sometimes whole baskets full. Every day he also brought to her a portion of the food he had prepared.

"There, Aderonke!" he said. "I hope you like this shellfish. I don't know what it is exactly, but it tastes good! Try a little of the pawpaw. Would you like some of these red berries?"

And every day he walked to the waterfall, carefully laid aside his feather cloak, and slipped into the pool with some gift for Aderonke's shrine. But he never put anything in the middle of the shelf.

Finally, on the last day of the festival, Remi rafted out to the cairn with two baskets of flowers and an especially large portion of food for Aderonke.

"See, Aderonke," he said, "I have brought you the very best of the food for this last day of the festival in your honor, and I have brought you many flowers— enough to make a bed for you if you like." Remi spread the flowers all around the cairn and heaped them in the crown as well.

Remi sat beside the cairn and chatted amiably to Aderonke, occasionally offering her a bite of dinner. When he was finished and the sun was getting low in the sky, he washed his hands and stood up.

"Now I have a special surprise for you, Aderonke!" he said. "This is the last day of your festival, and I have prepared for you a special song. I will sing it for you, but this song will last even when I am dead and can no longer sing for you. You see? I have written it down here on this scroll, and I will put it in your shrine tonight!"

## Then Remi began to sing the following lyrics:

Aderonke, Aderonke, Aderonke!
If Aderonke is with me, this is my home.
If Aderonke is with me, she is my family.
If Aderonke is with me, she is my heaven.
If Aderonke is with me, it does not matter
Whether I am alive or dead.

Aderonke, Aderonke, Aderonke!
If Aderonke is not with me, I am lost.
If Aderonke is not with me, I have no family.
If Aderonke is not with me, I am barred from
    heaven.
If Aderonke is not with me, it does not matter
Whether I am alive or dead.

Why am I cast away at the prime of our love?
Why am I cast away when I am about to win
    you?
Why am I cast away by the wickedness of
    others?
Why am I cast away to cry day and night?
Aderonke, Aderonke, Aderonke!
If I do not have Aderonke to love, I cannot
    love anyone.
If I do not have Aderonke to love, I shall
    never marry all my life.

If I do not have Aderonke to love, I have no
   life at all.

Aderonke, Aderonke, Aderonke!
You have changed my life for good.
Aderonke, Aderonke, Aderonke!
I will always love only you.
Aderonke, Aderonke, Aderonke!
I will cherish your memory forever.

Why is life so merciless?
Why do the evil suitors triumph?
Why do the thugs try to kill the innocent?
Why does the sea carry away the lover?

Life befriends the rich and casts away the
   poor.
Life befriends the wicked and casts away the
   innocent.
Life befriends the crooked and casts away the
   trustworthy.
Life befriends the thugs and casts away the
   lover.
Why is life so merciless?
Why do the evil suitors triumph?
Do they think I will forget my Aderonke?
Do they think I will not remember my Aderonke?

Aderonke, Aderonke, Aderonke!
You are my life to me.
You are my life to me.
I want no other life than Aderonke.
I have no other life than Aderonke.
Aderonke has given me a purpose in life.
Aderonke has given me a mission in life.

Without Aderonke, I would have drowned.
Without Aderonke, I would have died of thirst.
Without Aderonke, I would have succumbed.
Without Aderonke, I would be long dead.

You are my life to me, Aderonke.
Never forget me, Aderonke!
Always remember me, Aderonke!

Here I have made a place for you.
Here I have built a home for you.
Here I have raised a monument to you.
Here I have decked a shrine for you.
Here I have declared a festival for you.
Here I have written this song for you.
I have loved you in my life.
I will love you in my death.
I will love you after my death.

We will be together, Aderonke.
We will be together someday.
We will be together, Aderonke,
And I will love you forever.

When Remi finished singing, he rolled up the scroll and returned to shore on the raft. He walked up the forest path to the waterfall, removed his feather cloak, and carefully wrapped the scroll in a large leaf. Then he quickly ducked under the waterfall and placed the scroll in the center of the little shelf.

All the way home, he sang the song over and over, very softly.

#  SEVEN

That night Remi dreamed of Aderonke.

She was in a great tower, such as Remi had never seen in his life. It appeared to reach as high as the flight of the greatest birds. It was certainly taller than any of the buildings in the capital, but it had no windows on the sides and only one massive door. At the very top was a sort of porch, and Aderonke was standing on the porch looking down.

Below her, standing guard at the door, were her parents and her black dog. But now the dog was taller than the people, and he had a golden chain around his neck. Her father carried a long spear. This was strange because Remi could never remember having seen Aderonke's father carrying any sort of weapon or even wearing any of the traditional clothing of his people; rather, he preferred European clothing and was highly citified in his ways. In Remi's dream, however, both of Aderonke's parents were dressed in more traditional attire.

The tower stood in the middle of a great river. There were steps immediately outside the door, and this is where Aderonke's parents and dog were situated, with the current of the mighty stream swirling around them. There was no bridge to either shore, but this did not seem to be of any concern to the couple or the dog. What did seem to be of concern to them was the crowd of people who were trying to reach the tower.

At first, Remi could see only that there were what looked like hundreds of people on both shores, and they were crowding near the edge of the water. Then he noticed that one man had climbed a tall palm tree with a length of rope. This man kept throwing the rope and trying to grab hold of the edge of the porch where Aderonke was standing. The rope seemed to be well weighted, and at each throw, Remi held his breath. He was certain that this man must not reach Aderonke by any means.

Then Remi's attention turned to a boat coming upriver. This boat would approach the tower and then for some unaccountable reason veer off. It would approach again, nearly reach the steps, and then be caught in a current and sent spinning sideways toward the shore. Over and over again, this boat attempted an approach, but over and over again, it was unable to pull up to the steps.

Two other people were attempting to build a bridge, but the river current seemed quite swift, and they were having trouble getting the project under way. Nevertheless, they appeared to be making some slow progress, and it was these people who were being most closely watched by Aderonke's parents and her dog.

Suddenly, Remi (who now seemed to be down in the crowd himself) saw the people scramble to make way for someone who was coming: the town police officer.

"I will restore order here!" the police officer shouted in his most official voice. "Everybody, get out! Go home! I will have order now, or I will haul you all to the jail!"

*That's silly*, Remi thought. *He can't haul all these people to jail. Our little jail could hold only four people at best! And besides, there are so many of us...*

...The scene changed. He was above the tower somehow and very close to it. He could look down at Aderonke on the little porch, but she was not looking up at him. She was taking objects out of baskets and putting them back, folding lengths of cloths and unfolding them, stacking items up and unstacking them. Remi could see into the tower to a room full of baskets, boxes, and stacks of various objects. Aderonke looked very tired, as if she had been doing this for a long time.

"Aderonke!" he called. "Aderonke, look! I'm up here!"

Aderonke tilted her head and looked upward, but she showed no sign of recognizing Remi at all. Then she shrugged her shoulders and went back to her work, always keeping an eye out for the crowd on the shore.

"Aderonke!" Remi called again, but she did not respond.

Remi woke in a cold sweat. *My other dreams were true,* he thought. *Well, except for the one about Aderonke running across the sand, but maybe that one was true, too. Perhaps she is with me in spirit because I have built her a monument.*

Remi spent a long time out by the cairn that day, talking with his statue of Aderonke.

"I hope you are not a prisoner somewhere, Aderonke," he said. "Surely your parents would never do that to you, and you are too good to be in jail. What could that tower mean? And all those people? Have you done something that would make so many people angry with you? I don't see how that could be. Everybody likes you."

Remi looked out to sea and thought, *Could Aderonke be in some kind of danger? Something*

*the police would have to protect her from? And if*
*she is in trouble, what can I do about it?*

That night Remi dreamed again.

This dream was the most confusing yet. As it began, Remi could hear himself talking.

"I certainly am serious," he said. "Nobody can get something for nothing. Whoever tries the hardest will win her."

Remi could not see himself; in fact, he could not see anyone very clearly. One moment, he would seem to be near a woman sitting on a mat, and the next moment, he seemed to be standing outside someone's house. The scene was always vague, however, and he could never be certain exactly where he was.

"I hope no one hurts her," some older woman was saying. "These young men are proud, and I am certain some of them are going to be angry when she marries someone else. After all, she can marry only one man! And we have only this one daughter! You do not know how we longed to have more children, but only this one was apportioned to us! What would I do were someone to hurt my only child?"

"We can assist him with prayer, and if he is the right man for her, no one will be able to prevent it," another woman said. Was that Bimpe?

Then there were girls chanting the following:

> If you marry a sailor,
> If you marry a sailor,
> If you marry a sailor,
> Know for sure that
> He may be mad at you one day
> And drown you at sea!
> If you marry a sailor!

And before they stopped singing, he could hear a voice he certainly recognized. It was the pharmacist, and he said, "...other medication in the shop. I believe my assistant forgot to wrap it with the others."

He heard girls singing again:

> If you marry a pharmacist,
> If you marry a pharmacist,
> If you marry a pharmacist,
> Know for sure that
> He may be mad at you one day
> And splash acid on you!
> If you marry a pharmacist!

"Who is this fellow?" Remi was sure that voice belonged to the police officer.

"Her family has progressed beyond that sort of thing, and she needs to marry better," a young woman said.

"I have better manners than some people, and my hands are clean," Remi said.

"Not marry! But that is unheard of! What sort of foolish notions does the girl have?"

"How can she get over Remi with these suitors standing around all the time? She cannot leave her own house." Who was that? Aderonke's mother?

For a while there was no sound at all, only a confusion of colors. Then Remi heard, as from a great distance, what sounded like many women chanting over and over:

She's pining away!
She's pining away!
She's pining away!
Poor Aderonke is pining away!

Then there was a terrible noise, a loud "whump-whump!" The sound repeated over and over and over. It was such a racket Remi wanted only to wake up, but he could not. Wind was rushing about his ears, and he thought he would be knocked down. *But I can't be,* he thought, *because I'm really lying down dreaming.*

Instead of waking up, Remi saw something being moved past him in the dark. It looked like a bed of some kind, with someone on it. The person was all wrapped up in a dark blanket. Remi strained to determine who was in the blanket, but the harder he tried to see, the less he was able to.

Remi awoke, still straining his eyes to see through the darkness.

It was not yet light on the island, and Remi was surprised to be awake. In fact, he wondered at first if this wasn't still part of his dream. . But as the sky began to lighten a little, he was convinced his dream was over, particularly because he heard no more voices or strange noises.

He tried to recall exactly what each person had said in the dream, but the voices all seemed to run together. He knew that he himself had spoken in the dream, and he was sure these were statements he had actually uttered in the past. Was the dream only a confusion of memories?

But then again, he had never been in the center of such a dreadful noise! It seemed somehow vaguely familiar, but he could not quite place the sound. In any event, he knew he had not been that close to it if he had indeed heard it before. And the raging wind! What did that mean?

He could remember the women chanting about Aderonke pining away. For him? Did she miss him that much? Or was he simply hoping Aderonke missed him that much? That must be it. Heaven knew Aderonke had plenty of suitors, and if she thought Remi was dead, she would surely marry one of them.

That day Remi walked up to his little waterfall grotto and spent a long time staring into the pool. He stayed so late that he forgot to eat supper, and when he lay down to sleep that night, he did not notice the hunger, but he felt a terrible weight in his heart.

Remi dreamed again of the great tower.

The waters of the river were far wilder than before, as if there was a storm. The bridge builders had almost succeeded in crossing to the tower, however, and many people had joined them in a feverish effort to complete the bridge. The boat that had been trying to reach the tower had grown so that now it was almost a fourth as tall as the tower itself. It butted up against the steps where Aderonke's parents waited.

The big black dog was leaping and snarling, running back and forth along the edge of the steps.

Aderonke's father was holding his spear in readiness, waiting for the gangplank of the huge boat to be let down. He obviously intended to kill whoever was going to come down the gangplank, but what if there were too many for him?

Worse yet, Remi could see that the man who had previously climbed the palm tree had done so again. This time, he had a longer rope and a better weight. Again and again he threw, and finally the weight slipped over the railing of the porch on which Aderonke stood. The man pulled the rope taut and anchored it to the tree.

Aderonke shrank back against the wall and then disappeared into the tower.

The man with the rope fastened another rope around his waist and looped it around the rope bridge. Then he let himself down and began to go hand over hand across the rope bridge. He was headed straight for Aderonke's little porch.

He was well over the water when Remi saw Bimpe come out onto the porch with a machete. She started hacking on the rope to cut it, but the rope was thick, and the machete seemed to be dull. The more she hacked at it, the thicker the rope seemed to get.

Meanwhile, the gangplank had come down from the boat. Aderonke's dog stood at the bottom snarling and snapping, and a man in a fancy uniform appeared at the top.

The water was bouncing the boat around, however, and the man in the uniform stood at the top of the gangplank looking undecided about whether he should brave both the dog and the spear while unsteady on his feet.

Just as the man in the uniform decided he should make a rush for it, Remi could see that the man on the rope was now only a few feet from the tower. Bimpe was hacking ferociously at the rope, and Aderonke's father was shouting something at the man on the gangplank, but it appeared that they could not hold out much longer.

Then Remi heard the mysterious sound: Whump-whump! Whump-whump!

There was a great wind, and the man on the rope struggled to maintain his hold. The man on the gangplank struggled to maintain his footing. The bridge builders struggled to keep from being swept into the water.

Then Remi saw where the odd sound was coming from—and the wind as well. An enormous bird with blue and white feathers had appeared, and it circled the tower. This bird was far larger than even the boat, and it made the tower itself look only average in height. The people on the riverbanks screamed and began to run away from the river, trampling one another as they retreated.

With each flap of the bird's wings, Remi heard the "whump-whump!" sound and felt another blast of wind, although he could not tell whether he himself was on the ground or somewhere suspended in the air or even in the tower itself.

"Run!" Aderonke's father shouted to his wife. "Run into the tower!"

She ran to the door and pushed it open. "Come quickly!" she cried. "While you have the chance!"

Perhaps Aderonke's father thought the bird a greater menace than the man in the uniform, but he did as she said. The great black dog remained snarling and barking on the steps, refusing to go in.

The man on the rope was now struggling desperately to keep from falling, and the danger seemed to give him new strength. But just as the man reached the railing of the porch, the bird reached down and snapped the rope in two with its enormous beak. The man lost his balance and fell into the raging water.

The bird circled the tower again, and Remi could feel his heart pounding with the fear that the bird would destroy the tower and Aderonke with it. He felt helpless with terror, and for all he had experienced, Remi had never been so frightened in his life. His own life meant nothing, but Aderonke's meant everything!

The repetitious "whump-whump!" sound grew louder and louder. It became unbearably loud. Remi covered his ears—whether in his dream or in reality, he did not know—and braced himself against the terrible wind. He watched in terror as the bird swooped down and knocked the porch off the tower. It reached into the tower with one giant claw, all the time beating its wings fiercely. (The "whump-whump!" noises grew deafening.) The bird's claw brought out the limp and lifeless form of Aderonke. The bird clutched her to its breast and rose on a spiral of wind....

"Aderonke!" Remi screamed. "Aderonke!"

He awoke screaming Aderonke's name over and over. His throat was raw from screaming. His hands were clutched tight over his ears, and his heart was beating wildly.

Remi had never experienced such a nightmare. It had all seemed so real, and nothing about it seemed particularly fantastic other than the bird. Even the bird had not seemed fantastic—but merely terrifying—while he was dreaming it. All about this dream was an air of reality, even though he knew Aderonke was not in a tower. There was no such large river within a hundred miles of their town. Aderonke's father never dressed like that or carried a spear. No one would try to build a wooden bridge in a raging river. Aderonke's dog did not wear a golden chain around his neck, especially not a golden chain as big around as a man's arm. Nevertheless, everything in the dream seemed real.

Remi sat up, shaking. It couldn't be true. It was just a dream.

He felt a twinge of hunger. Perhaps he should get something to eat. Remi slowly climbed down his ladder and made his way on wobbly legs to the pawpaw tree. The first few bites made him ravenous, and he remembered that he had had no supper the night before.

Maybe that was it. He had been extremely hungry, and his hunger took the first dream and twisted it to frightening proportions. But he had been hungry plenty of times before, and never had he had such a nightmare.

When he had stopped shaking and his hunger was satiated, Remi swam slowly out to the reef.

"Aderonke," he said, "I need to know what is going on. I have dreamed of you for three nights, and each dream is more confusing than the one before. I cannot make any sense out of it, and you see what a state I'm in! Look at me!" He spread his arms out dramatically. "I can't understand it. We were so happy just three days ago. I know you were pleased with your festival. Now I can't remember to eat, and my heart pounds in my ears. What's wrong?"

Remi huddled against the cairn almost the whole day; he looked like a sick child huddled against his mother. The sun beat down on his back, and the tide rose and fell, but Remi stayed motionless.

When Remi eventually rose from that place, it was with a new resoluteness in the set of his shoulders. He dove into the reef water and caught a substantial supper for himself, which he cooked immediately. He gathered a coconut, three yams, and several pieces of fruit and settled down by the fire to wait for supper. He would not go to bed on an empty stomach tonight.

He felt calmer after spending the day out by the monument, but he was also disturbed. Nothing had been normal since the festival. Remi wondered, *Was it possible that something in the festival had not been right? Could Aderonke be displeased?*

Then again, the opposite was a possibility, too. Perhaps Aderonke had been quite pleased and was trying to send him some sort of message through his dreams.

Either way, he knew the dreams were important somehow. He would have to find out the truth of them.

There was no point in mooning around. He resolved to carry out his usual duties—Aderonke would certainly be displeased with him if he grew careless—and put his trust in prayer and Aderonke's goodness. She would help him solve the problem.

After his supper, Remi took a torch and went up to the waterfall. He stayed there for a long time, praying for an answer to the meaning of the dreams. If Aderonke was displeased with him, he would be glad to do anything to please her. If she was trying to send him a message, he wanted to know what it was.

With a peaceful heart, Remi lay down to sleep at last.

The next morning when Remi awoke, he was extremely disoriented. He was certain he should be dreaming, and it took him a while to realize that he was in his own tree house, wide awake. He could not remember having dreamed at all. *Well,* he thought, *I will trust Aderonke. I know the answer will come to me when it is time.*

That day Remi set about seeing if he could separate the fibers of the lianas and make some pliable items that would be useful to him. He needed a net to snare birds, and he wanted to see if he could weave some kind of cloth. He had to do some experimenting with the materials at hand.

Eventually, Remi found one kind of liana that had rather thin, soft fibers without the sharp edges so common on most of them. He cut several lengths with his abalone-shell machete and spent much of the afternoon separating and knotting the fibers.

"What do you think?" he asked when he went out for his daily conversation at Aderonke's monument. "Do you think this is going to hold for a net? You know, I'd like to catch one of those parrots—the kind with the long, blue-and-gold tail—and keep it for a pet. I've heard you can teach them to talk." He was silent for a moment. "It might be best to take one from the nest. That way it would be so young, it would think I was its mother, and it would be easy to tame. Well, we'll see."

Three uneventful days passed, and three nights passed without dreams. Remi finished constructing his net and made an excursion to the marsh. He tried the net on several birds, letting each one go after he caught it because he did not need it for food and had no particular use for the feathers at the moment. He adjusted the weights and retied some of the knots, changing the design until he had exactly what he wanted. This net would have to be able to bring down a strong flier.

He looked all around for a parrot family, but none was near the marsh. He would have to look around the forest.

After four days of trouncing through the forest with his neck craned upward, Remi spotted a parrot family with nestlings. The babies were quite funny looking, but he could tell what colors they would be when they grew up. Getting close to them took more patience, as both of the parents stayed fairly close to the nest. It was a large clutch, however—four growing chicks—and both parents were hard pressed to keep them fed. As a result, Remi knew that both of them would be away from the nest at one time or another.

Remi's caution was occasioned by the size of the adult parrots' beaks. They could snap the fingers of his hand in an instant, and he had no doubt that they would fight with their claws as well. He supposed that when he removed a baby from the nest, the chick would give him a brave nip, but he didn't want to take any chances with angry parents.

Finally, Remi had his opportunity. The chicks were quiet, and the parents went off together on a flight around the neighborhood. Remi was a little surprised at this because it looked for all the world like a mating flight. These parents were apparently ready to raise another family, and he was just in time to take one of the earlier clutch.

He climbed quickly to the nest and clamped his hand over the sleeping chick. Remi was astonished that the chick neither struggled nor bit at his hand. It remained passive, simply scrambling with his claws to gain a purchase on something.

It was a fuzzy little creature, with its infant feathers sticking out in all directions, but Remi could tell it was going to be a beauty. Remi climbed down carefully from the nest, holding the baby bird to his chest and making soothing noises.

He took the bird home to his tree house and kept it in a basket while he fashioned a cage for it. Of course, the bird would be able to bite its way out of the cage with that great beak, but Remi's instincts told him that the bird would want something to call "home" just as he did. He tried to make the inside of the cage as much like the chick's birthnest as possible. Then he put the bird—basket and all—into the cage. The bird was awake now, but it didn't seem particularly alarmed. It watched Remi first out of one round eye and then the other, cocking its head and raising its infant crest in apparent curiosity.

"Come along, bird," Remi said. "We are going for a little ride." Remi carried the cage out to the raft and poled across the reef waters to Aderonke's monument. "There now, you're going to meet your mistress!" he said with excitement.

He gently lifted the cage from the raft and set it down by the monument. "Look, Aderonke!" Remi said. "I have brought you a friend. Isn't he beautiful? I've no idea whether it's a male or a female, but I've got to name it something. What do you think?"

For some time, Remi leaned against the cairn, making baby-bird sounds to the chick and occasionally addressing a remark to Aderonke. He took the chick from its cage and stroked its feathers, helping it to balance on his wrist. "What shall I call you?" he asked, but the chick only tilted its head and gazed at him with one eye.

"I know!" Remi cried suddenly, startling the poor bird into flopping off his wrist and blundering around on the sand. "Waterfall!"

Remi carefully picked the bird up and soothed it against his chest. "Waterfall. That's what I'll call you because you will have beautiful, long blue feathers with gold in them and because you will learn to sing the song in praise of Aderonke."

When they returned to the island, Remi made a tiny jess of the liana fiber for Waterfall's foot, so the bird would not accidentally fall and hurt himself or manage to fly away. When Waterfall rode on Remi's wrist, Remi kept the jess very short; when he rode on Remi's shoulder, he lengthened the jess. Inside the tree house, the jess was completely removed.

In a few days, Waterfall had matured enough to be able to fly a little. Remi lengthened the jess and let Waterfall fly as far as he could, and he trained the bird to always return to him for a reward of food.

During all this time of hunting, capturing, and training Waterfall, Remi had no dreams that he could remember. He awoke rested every morning and felt certain that the meaning of the dreams would be made clear to him.

# EIGHT

Waterfall quickly grew into a large bird, and his tail was as long as Remi's arm. His favorite perch was Remi's shoulder, and eventually Remi was certain enough of Waterfall's tameness that he removed the jess. The only time they were apart at all was when Remi went swimming, and then Waterfall would fly out to Aderonke's monument and perch on it, squawking the whole time for Remi to hurry up and come out of the water.

Despite his excellent flying abilities, Waterfall seldom flew about; he seemed content to stay with Remi even when other birds of his kind were nearby. Remi was glad of this. Remi had thought that Waterfall might join his fellows when he had the chance, but the parrot seemed uninterested in other birds except to imitate their calls. In fact, he imitated everything he heard. Remi was astonished one morning to be awakened by a sort of roar very close to his head. His heart nearly stopped in terror. He had not seen any mammals on the island at all and could not imagine what sort of large predator had discovered his home. When his eyes adjusted to the dim light of dawn, he discovered that it was only Waterfall growling. It took Remi some time to realize that what Waterfall was imitating was the roll of the surf!

Remi was pleased at this development because it meant that Waterfall would probably learn Aderonke's special song easily. Remi tried singing the whole song to Waterfall over and over, but the bird did not seem to understand that he could sing it himself. Finally, Remi tried repeating just the first line, which of course was Aderonke's name: "Aderonke, Aderonke, Aderonke!"

At first, Waterfall seemed to pick up only the sounds of the tones in Remi's voice, but it was not long before he was able to sing the first line recognizably.

Remi was so happy with this that he swam out to the cairn and had Waterfall show off his new talent.

"Listen, Aderonke," he said, patting the monument. "Waterfall has learned to sing your name!"

And Waterfall obediently sang the first line of Aderonke's song: "Aderonke, Aderonke, Aderonke!"

Then began many months of training for Waterfall. Remi found that although the bird could imitate many different sounds, he could learn only four or five notes at a time. Sometimes Remi had to break one line of the song into two halves and teach each half to Waterfall separately; when Waterfall learned both halves, Remi showed the bird how to sing them together. Waterfall seemed to enjoy his singing lessons and did very well with them. The only problem was that Waterfall enjoyed them so much that he liked to play with the parts of the song that he had learned—jumbling them up, making up nonsensical things to go with them, and so on. This distressed Remi at first, but then he decided that Waterfall was simply adding his own twist to the chant and that this, too, was a gift for Aderonke.

One day Remi and Waterfall were out on the reef near Aderonke's cairn. Remi was lying in the sand, and Waterfall was perched on the cairn. Waterfall looked at Remi critically. Suddenly, the bird took off and began to fly.

"Aderonke, Aderonke, Aderonke!" he cried as he ascended into the sky.

Remi jumped up and called him frantically. He was afraid that Waterfall would fly away and never come back. "Waterfall, come back here! Come to Remi!"

But Waterfall was flying in ever-widening circles around the monument. He did not fly very high, and all the time he cried part of Aderonke's song:

Aderonke, Aderonke, Aderonke!
If Aderonke is with me, this is my home.
If Aderonke is with me, she is my family.
If Aderonke is with me, she is my heaven.
If Aderonke is with me, it does not matter
Whether I am alive or dead.

Waterfall seemed to settle into a pattern he liked, traveling around and around in a circle that did not reach all the way to the beach. He was about as far off the surface of the water as the top of a palm tree would be from the ground, and all the time he called over and over again, "Aderonke, Aderonke, Aderonke! If Aderonke is with me, this is my home."

After he had flown around Remi and the monument eight times this way, Waterfall flew straight to Remi and settled on his shoulder. Remi took him on his wrist and talked to him.

"What is the matter with you, Waterfall? I have never seen you make such a flight before. You wouldn't leave me now, would you, when you have learned so much of Aderonke's song and when you are my only companion?"

Waterfall just cocked his head and looked at Remi out of one eye. He did not fly again that day except to cross the water to the beach when it was time to go home.

That night Remi had a dream.

In Remi's dream, Waterfall was flying around in circles, calling Aderonke's name, and singing a part of the song that he had not yet actually learned:

We will be together, Aderonke.
We will be together someday.
We will be together, Aderonke,
And I will love you forever.

As Remi watched, Waterfall left behind him in the air a sort of reddish streak, and when he had made a full circle, the red streak remained in the air. It was a red circle against the blue sky. Waterfall flew around this red circle eight times, and he repeated that verse of Aderonke's song each time.

When he had completed the eight circuits, Waterfall grew very large, almost as large as the circle itself, and he flew to the center of it and hovered—something that in real life he could not do well at all. For some reason, he looked familiar, not like

Waterfall at all but like something else Remi had seen before. Then the circle of red became a circle of red blossoms in the air, and as they fell to the ground, Remi heard a sound he had heard only in his dreams: "Whump-whump! Whump-whump!"

Waterfall settled down in the center of the circle of flowers, and the "whump-whump!" got louder and louder. Then as Waterfall folded his wings, the sound stopped.

Then Remi became aware of his feet. He was standing on the ring of petals, and he was holding a wreath of large red and yellow flowers. He could hear himself chanting, and he could hear Waterfall chanting, too:

> Here I have made a place for you.
> Here I have made a home for you.
> Here I have raised a monument to you.
> Here I have decked a shrine for you.
> Here I have declared a festival for you.
> Here I have written this song for you.

This is when Remi woke up, and Waterfall was happily singing Aderonke's song to the morning sun.

Remi was thoughtful all that day. He took Waterfall out to the cairn, but he didn't talk to Aderonke.

He just stared out to sea and thought about his dreams. What was that "whump-whump!" that kept reappearing? He could vaguely remember having heard such a sound at some point in his past life—that's how he thought of the time before he came to the island—but he could not remember exactly what it was. It must be important; it must have something to do with Aderonke.

Then there was the circle. He remembered the dream he had had the night he washed up on the reef, how he had seen himself standing on the flower petals and holding a wreath. What was he doing with that wreath? Putting it on something stone....Of course! It was the monument to Aderonke! And, in fact, he had put many similar wreaths on that cairn in the past few months. He couldn't remember if the flower petals were in a circle in that earlier dream. No, they couldn't have been because he was looking out toward the sea and Aderonke was running toward him. But he had felt the same flowers under his feet.

And then the bird. Waterfall had made the great red circle that fell to the earth as flowers, and Waterfall was helping Remi chant Aderonke's song. But he had grown so big—like that giant bird in Remi's dream of the tower, the one that had swooped down and taken Aderonke away. Would Waterfall hurt Aderonke? Of course not. He would love Aderonke just as Remi did. And Waterfall could not carry Aderonke....

For a moment, Remi was lost in a fantasy. He envisioned Waterfall flying across the ocean, picking Aderonke up in his talons, and carrying her to the island. How lovely that would be! They could live here forever without having to worry about that vicious little pharmacist and all the other suitors.

Was it the bird's wings that made the "whump-whump" noise? Remi shook his head. Nothing seemed to make sense, but he was certain there was a meaning in these dreams. It was if he could feel Aderonke reaching out to him, trying to tell him something.

What was he missing? Reaching out...it had something to do with reaching out. Remi closed his eyes and pictured the great parrot flying around in the circle, the circle of flowers....Where had he seen such a circle of flowers before? No, it wasn't flowers, but it was red. A red circle.

"That's it!" Remi cried, jumping up and startling poor Waterfall so that he fell off the cairn and fluttered about for a moment before settling down on the sand a few feet from Remi.

"Aderonke, Aderonke, Aderonke!" he squawked.

"That's right, Waterfall!" Remi said joyfully. "Come here. Get up on my shoulder. I'm going to tell you about something wonderful!"

Waterfall came, his head cocked as if expecting Remi to jump around strangely again. But he settled on Remi's shoulder readily enough, adding his own comment:

> Aderonke has given me a purpose in life.
> Aderonke has given me a mission in life.
> Aderonke, Aderonke, Aderonke!

"Waterfall, you are a wise bird!" Remi remarked. "Let me tell you all about the circle of flowers that you showed me in my dream. How can I ever thank you for showing me this?" He nuzzled Waterfall's beak with his chin and began to explain to the bird everything he knew about the circle of flowers.

Remi was not perfectly certain about how to go about what he had in mind, but he was perfectly certain that he was going to do it somehow.

Before he could even begin to gather flowers, Remi wanted to be sure the design was correct. For the next few weeks, he spent most of his time on the beach, marking out circles in the sand. He tried the largest circle he could manage, thinking that perhaps the size Waterfall had first shown him was the best, but it didn't seem right at all. He tried very small circles so that he could be close to all parts of the circle at once, but these didn't seem right either.

After each try, he would discuss the matter with Waterfall. "How about this?" Remi would ask, but each time Waterfall would merely turn his head and look at the project with a critical eye. Then Remi would obliterate the circle and try another.

He finally decided on a circle that was exactly as wide as he was tall with his hands held over his head. He could mark this out easily in the sand by simply lying down and stretching as far as he could reach. Somehow this had the right "feel" to it.

The size of the circle was only part of his planning, however. The circle also had to be in the right place.

Remi was certain that the circle should be on the beach because he remembered how he had felt the sand under his feet in the first dream. But the cairn had been in that dream, too, so there was the possibility that the circle should be somewhere on the reef, perhaps even with the cairn in the middle of it. He spent several frustrated days moving the location up and down the beach and finding places on the reef where it might fit, as the part of the barrier that was above the water was not very wide in most places. He discovered that Aderonke's monument was on too narrow a strip of coral and sand for the circle to be anywhere near it.

At last, Remi hit on the idea of lining up his circle with the rising sun. *After all,* he told himself, *Aderonke is the sun to me.* Again, this felt "right," but when he asked Waterfall for comments, the bird was stubbornly silent.

But Waterfall had something to learn before the circle could be made. He had to learn the last part of the song so that he could sing it with Remi. Everything on this occasion would have to be perfect.

Waterfall could not sing the whole song all by himself, though he could sing snatches of it on his own. But he could sing the entire song along with Remi, and he seemed to enjoy doing so. It was not long before Waterfall was able to sing the whole song with Remi; they practiced it every day, while Remi worked on a new song that he would sing himself.

There were always flowers of some sort on the island, but now Remi was beginning to get used to the rhythm with which they changed from month to month. He was waiting for a certain medium-sized red flower. It was rather plain and had a slight pinkish cast to it; its fragrance was almost overpowering; and it opened its blossoms as soon as the sun came up. These blossoms would last only until about noon and then wither, but their fragrance lingered until after sunset. When Remi had smelled them close up on other occasions, they had made his head swim. He felt that this type of intoxicating scent was exactly what was needed in this instance.

There was also a matter of symbols and patterns. He knew that the circle should contain some special designs, but he did not know what these were, as he had never seen this done before. He had to invent his own patterns, but he wanted to be sure they were right. He watched the sky for omens, prayed every night for some kind of sign in his dreams, and kept a careful eye on Waterfall in case the bird should give him some hint.

Remi eventually settled on his design. It would incorporate a portrait of Waterfall because the bird seemed somehow to belong in the middle of the circle and to be connected with the "whump-whump!" sound of his dreams. Also, there would be the writing paper and pen Remi had given Aderonke, a likeness of her big black dog, and as careful a representation of her doorpost as Remi could devise.

Remi drew the design over and over in the sand with a stick, adjusting various parts of it, until he got it exactly right. When he had finally arranged it correctly, some parts were no longer recognizable to a casual observer because they had undergone some changes to make the design look "right." This did not bother Remi, however, because he had a sense of being guided in his work. And whenever Remi drew in the sand, Waterfall ceased his constant chatter and watched silently.

The completed design had some parts in it that Remi himself did not understand, but they had a feeling of "rightness" about them, so he left them in.

When the red blossoms came into bloom, Remi carefully marked out the spot where the circle would be at sunup the following morning. Because the plant the blossoms grew on was a vine that hung on practically every nearby tree, Remi knew he would have no trouble gathering enough of them to do the job. He also picked out a supply of tiny blue flowers and some larger golden ones because he had decided that the part of the design representing Waterfall should be done in Waterfall's own colors.

Remi was a little concerned that he might not wake up early enough, so he went to bed very early in hopes of waking early. He need not have worried, however, because he simply didn't sleep at all that night. He spent the hours going over and over his plans in his head, perfecting his new chant, and arranging flower petals on an imaginary beach.

When the first light came, Remi and Waterfall were out of the tree house and gathering blossoms. Remi gathered a large basketful of the red flowers and a small basketful of the blue and gold ones. He judged that there was plenty of time, so before he headed for the beach, he walked up to Aderonke's shrine and prayed that his efforts might be successful. He washed himself clean in Aderonke's pool and walked back to the beach naked and without any ornaments on his body.

There Remi carefully laid out a circle of the red blossoms, quite thick and intoxicatingly fragrant. Having constructed his design so many times in his head during the night, he was able to do so quickly on the sand this morning. When he was finished, the entire inside of the circle was filled with colorful petals in an interlocking pattern of red, blue, and gold.

As the first rays of the sun began to peek over the horizon, just above Aderonke's monument, Remi and Waterfall started to sing Aderonke's song:

Aderonke, Aderonke, Aderonke!
If Aderonke is with me, this is my home.
If Aderonke is with me, she is my family.
If Aderonke is with me, she is my heaven.
If Aderonke is with me, it does not matter
Whether I am alive or dead.

Aderonke, Aderonke, Aderonke!
If Aderonke is not with me, I am lost.
If Aderonke is not with me, I have no family.
If Aderonke is not with me, I am barred from
  heaven.
If Aderonke is not with me, it does not matter
Whether I am alive or dead.

Why am I cast away at the prime of our love?
Why am I cast away when I am about to win
   you?
Why am I cast away by the wickedness of
   others?
Why am I cast away to cry day and night?
Aderonke, Aderonke, Aderonke!

Waterfall seemed to enjoy this performance immensely. He added chirps and squawks and trills and occasional cries of "Aderonke!" between the lines. Remi had fasted the entire day before, and the fragrance of the flowers was making him more than a little woozy. Despite the seriousness of the occasion, he was amused by the antics of the parrot and had to stop himself several times from laughing out loud.

When they had finished their song, the sun was above the monument. Then Remi began to chant the song he had been working on in his head:

We will bring Aderonke near to us.
We will bring Aderonke near to us.
We will bring Aderonke to our circle!
Aderonke will come to our circle!
Aderonke will come to our island!

We will bring Aderonke near to us.
We will bring Aderonke near to us.
We will bring Aderonke into our sight!
Aderonke will come into our sight!
Aderonke will come to our island!

We will bring Aderonke near to us.
We will bring Aderonke near to us.
We will bring Aderonke with the sunrise!
Aderonke will come with the sunrise!
Aderonke will come to our island!

Come now, Aderonke, come and let me see you!
Come now, Aderonke, come and let me see you!
Come now, Aderonke, explain my dreams to me!
Come now, Aderonke, tell me what you have to
    say!
Aderonke, Aderonke, Aderonke!

(At this point, the parrot joined in joyfully, sing-
    ing Aderonke's song in snatches, but Remi
    did not mind. He was too intent on what he
    himself was doing.)

You are my Aderonke; I am your Remi!
You are my wife; I am your husband!
Come now, Aderonke, come and let me see you!
Come now, Aderonke, come and let me see you!

You are my sun; I can see by your light!

You are my sun; you show me everything!

Come now, Aderonke, explain my dreams to me!

Come now, Aderonke, tell me what you have to
   say!

You are my Aderonke; I am your Remi!

You are my wife; I am your husband!

You want to tell me something; your Remi is listening!

You want to show me something; your Remi is
   watching!

Come now, Aderonke, come and let me see you!

Come now, Aderonke, come and let me see you!

Remi went on like this at great length, and as he sang, his head swam more and more. He was standing up, but he found he could not keep his balance properly after a while, and he tried to sit down. As he did so, he stumbled into the red ring of flower petals and felt them under his feet. He dropped to his knees inside the circle and blinked his eyes hard, trying to focus them.

Now Remi could hear his own voice, still chanting, but a long way off. He could also hear Waterfall merrily singing the Aderonke song, but he no longer recognized the bird's voice. And once again, Remi could hear the repetitious "whump-whump!" he had heard in his dreams.

He blinked his eyes again, and as he focused them on the design in front of him, it began to move.

Remi saw three women—his own mother, Aderonke's mother, and Bimpe—with their arms around one another, chanting the following:

*She's pining away!*
*She's pining away!*
*She's pining away!*
*Poor Aderonke is pining away!*

Then the women broke up in laughter, not at all worried about poor Aderonke pining away. Where was Aderonke? What was the matter with her? Remi tried to muster all his strength and put it into his desire to see Aderonke.

There she was! But she was lying in bed in a dark room. Eli and Bimpe had stopped laughing and were fanning Aderonke's brow and wiping it with wet cloths. "I am glad you came," she whispered. "I am so sorry....I'm tired." She smiled the tiniest of smiles, rolled her eyes up in her head, and was silent. Remi looked on in horror as Eli and Bimpe started laughing again.

With a sinking heart, he heard the "whump-whump!" getting louder and louder. What was wrong with Aderonke, and why were her mother and Bimpe laughing about it? And what *was* that thing that made the terrible noise?

Then Remi saw the outside of Aderonke's house. It was daytime, and there were quite a few young men hanging around. One of them was banging on the door, another was looking warily at Aderonke's dog, and a third was across the street watching what was going on. The pharmacist was coming up the street, and the police officer could be seen making his rounds. Remi saw Aderonke's house grow taller and taller. The tower! He knew her house was the tower!

Then it was night. He could hear the "whump-whump!" louder than ever. It was all he could hear. Even the sound of chanting had been washed out by this sinister sound. And he saw the bird—only it wasn't a bird at all.

Remi was certainly in a trance. He had intended the fasting, the fragrant blossoms, and the chanting to put him in exactly such a state, but the sight of the helicopter almost jolted him out of it. That was what had made the "whump-whump!" sound! He strained his eyes to see.

Someone bundled in a blanket was being carried into the helicopter. Remi was certain he knew who that someone was, and he was filled with grief, but he could not even call Aderonke's name.

He watched as the helicopter rose into the sky and again as it came down. He saw Aderonke's father get out of the helicopter, and he saw Aderonke herself carefully unloaded and gently carried into a big building. The helicopter rose into the air again, and the "whump-whump!" faded into the distance.

Remi was heartbroken and numb. Aderonke must be dying. Perhaps she was already dead. But why was her mother and the other women laughing about Aderonke "pining away"?

Remi could not move, nor could he feel the anger that he knew he should be feeling. How could anyone be so callous as to joke about Aderonke's being sick to death?

But as Remi watched, he saw a strange thing indeed. Even though it was still night, he could see Aderonke's father come out of the large building—with Aderonke following him! Her father had a big smile on his face, and Aderonke was giggling. She looked perfectly healthy to Remi. He tried to call her name, but he could not speak.

Then the flower petals seemed to move around again, and Remi saw Aderonke once more, this time very close up, as if he were sitting next to her. She was in a room that was obviously a city apartment. Remi could see another woman—someone perhaps ten years older than Aderonke—in the room with her. Two little boys around seven years old ran through the room shouting, and they banged their way out the door. The women were sitting at a table, drinking something out of teacups. On the table beside Aderonke was a stack of books.

"Why you want to go the university?" the woman asked. "I never thought of you as intellectually inclined."

"Oh, I'm not, Aunt Nimi," Aderonke answered. "In fact, I think it's strange that *you*_went to the university, and to be honest with you, I don't like the city much even though I lived here when I was younger. It's all very well for you with your husband in the government, but I prefer the village. But then…well, you know how it is."

"You won't go back."

"No, I won't go back. Remi has been murdered by those thugs. My father is convinced the pharmacist was behind it, but there isn't really any proof. And I am not going to marry the pharmacist or anyone else who might have been involved. Suppose it was really a whole gang of my suitors who did it?" Aderonke took a sip of her drink. "And I don't want to marry anyone at all now."

"Not ever?"

"Well, that's how I feel now. Twenty years from now, who knows? I'll tell you, Aunt Nimi, it was fun having all those suitors. I really enjoyed it, but I was just a child. I had no idea how serious the whole thing could get. And my foolishness cost Remi his life! That has left a bitter taste in my mouth. So I'm going to struggle through university classes and get a government job—your husband promised to help me—and live here in the city with no man at all."

"You will want children, Aderonke."

"Perhaps I will be a teacher. If I can't have Remi's children, I don't want those of any other man."

Remi did not actually faint, but he lay quiet in the circle of flowers for a long time before he came to his senses. Waterfall was still on his shoulder.

"Aderonke, Aderonke, Aderonke!" the bird sang.

Remi shook his head. "That's right, old friend. It was Aderonke. Now I know what my dreams meant." Remi stirred the wilting flower petals with his fingers. "And I don't know whether to laugh or cry."

For the next several days, Remi neither laughed nor cried. He was too busy thinking. Aderonke was certainly alive. Remi had no doubt about that. And she was no longer in the village. She had spoken of the university and of having lived in this city when she was younger, so she must be in the capital with Aunt Nimi. Aderonke's father's sister, Nimi was famous in the nearby villages because when she had been a little girl, she had pestered her brothers to teach her to read. One thing led to another, and somehow Nimi went off to the university. She was the first young woman in the district to have done so. And there she met her husband, a young man destined for an important government post.

What a stir that had caused! Nimi had always been so independent that her parents had never been able to arrange a betrothal for her; they were probably just as glad that Nimi had found a husband on her own! But her young suitor had a hard time convincing his family he should marry Nimi, who was nobody but a village girl and obviously too independent for her own good. The negotiations between the families were drawn out; the gossip was dreadful; and even the premier, who was a friend of the young man's family, had his say in the matter.

It had worked out well, though. Nimi earned her degree and settled down to help her husband with his political career. She was quite good looking (Remi thought she bore a strong resemblance to Aderonke) and very well spoken. She entertained important people graciously, got along well with Europeans and other foreigners with whom her husband dealt in his work, and presented him with twin sons the year after their marriage. The gossip died down, and the village was rather proud of Nimi, the local girl who had done well for herself and made good connections for her family. Those good connections were, in fact, one of the reasons for Aderonke's father's prestige in his village.

So now Aderonke was going to the university, too. Remi's heart sank at the thought. If Aderonke stayed at the university, might she not meet a husband? She said she did not want to marry, but wouldn't Remi fade into the back of her mind as she met other young men—educated young men with a future in government, science, or industry—at the university? Would she ever want to go back to the village with Remi?

Then again, what chance did Remi have of ever letting Aderonke know he was alive? He had not seen a single ship in all the months he had spent on the island. He finally gave up on the signal fire and let it burn out, keeping only a small firepit for his own cooking. He gradually made his tree house as commodious and comfortable as possible because it looked as if he was going to spend his entire life there. In short, Remi did not expect to ever see Aderonke again. Wouldn't it be better for her to settle in at the university and find a good husband? How could he expect her not to marry?

But Remi was alive. Part of Aderonke's song ran through Remi's mind over and over:

Life befriends the rich and casts away the
poor.
Life befriends the wicked and casts away the
innocent.
Life befriends the crooked and casts away the
trustworthy.
Life befriends the thugs and casts away the
lover.
Why is life so merciless?

Was he to spend his whole life on this island, forever separated from his true wife? Was Aderonke to spend her life husbandless and childless because of this twist of fate? Or was she to marry some other man, unaware that her own Remi was alive and longing for her?

While Remi thought long and hard about his uncertain future, Waterfall sat on his shoulder, chattering quietly and pulling lovingly on Remi's hair. Occasionally, Waterfall would cry out, "Aderonke! Aderonke! Aderonke!"

Waterfall did not try to sing more of Aderonke's song, though. Remi was grateful for this. It seemed to him as if the bird understood his distress and his need to ponder what he should do.

Having no one else to talk to other than his bird and his stone monument of Aderonke, Remi often responded to Waterfall's chattering.

"Oh, old bird," he said, "how I wish I could send you to Aderonke to pick her up like that bird in my dream and just carry her to me! We could live here forever and be happy, just us and our children—no university, no pharmacist, no palm-wine seller, no thugs, no rich parents and poor parents." And Remi patted the bird as if to comfort him, but Remi was the one who needed comforting.

Within a week, Remi began to have another kind of dream entirely. In these dreams, he could see only one person, and that one only dimly. It was as if everything was taking place at that time of the evening just before total darkness, when all shapes are indistinct and the eyes play tricks on people. The person seemed to be a man—at least if he was the one doing the chanting that Remi always heard in these dreams. He saw no other human beings in these dreams.

Sometimes the man was standing, but he usually seemed to be sitting on the ground, apparently motionless. Remi never caught a glimpse of his face, but sometimes he could make out the man's forearms, which were stretched out in front of him. They looked sinewy, perhaps the arms of an old man and probably not the arms of a young one. Remi could make out nothing of what the man might be wearing or of his surroundings, although he got the impression that there may be trees in the background.

Remi also couldn't make out a single word of the chanting. In some ways, it sounded familiar, but in other ways, it sounded as if it must be some language Remi did not understand. It was a language that Remi *almost* understood, but the understanding receded from him as quickly as he approached it.

These dreams had two notable features, however. One was their persistence. Sometimes Remi woke several times in one night, each time from one of these dreams. No two of them were exactly alike, but nothing eventful happened in them except for the chanting and the dim perception of an old man with his arms outstretched.

The other unusual aspect of the dreams—and the detail that made Remi certain they were important to him—was that he saw Waterfall in some of them. Unlike the other features of the dream, however, Waterfall was always his own bright blue-and-gold color. It was as if he carried his own sunlight with him. And Waterfall was always either emerging from between the arms of the old man or flying to them. Remi would be looking at the old man, dim in the gathering dark, and suddenly he would see Waterfall emerge from the darkness of the old man's body or fly into his arms and disappear into that same darkness. But never once did Remi hear Waterfall squawk, chatter, sing, or say any of the words in his growing vocabulary.

There was no question in Remi's mind that Waterfall was an unusual bird. Remi chose this baby from the nest because he was the prettiest—although they all looked funny at that half-bald stage—and seemed to be the most responsive. But even though Waterfall acted much like many other parrots with which Remi had been familiar over the years, Waterfall seemed to have a depth of intelligence that was not always birdlike. And he was undoubtedly connected with Aderonke in Remi's dreams. For this reason, Remi thought a great deal about the possible meaning of these recurring dreams. Waterfall had heard Remi ponder out loud about what to do. Were these dreams some sort of an answer to Remi's difficulty? And if they were, where were they coming from? Was Waterfall himself the dream sender? What of the old man? Who was he, and why would he send Remi a dream—a dream that told him nothing at all? Remi decided to ask Waterfall about the dreams.

One day as they sat on the beach looking out to sea, Remi spoke to Waterfall, who was gently tugging on Remi's hair. "Waterfall, I've got to have a serious talk with you. I have been getting these dreams over and over. They wake me in the middle of the night sometimes, and it is always the same sort of dream. It is almost dark, and I cannot see very well. There seems to be an old man—at least I don't think he's a very young man—and he may be chanting, though. I can't see for sure if he's the one who's chanting. He holds his arms out in front of him like this, and sometimes you fly out from between his arms or you fly from some other place to between his arms. Are you sending me these dreams, Waterfall? Are you trying to tell me something?"

Waterfall just tugged on Remi's hair. Remi waited patiently for Waterfall to tell him something, but the bird did not speak at all. He simply muttered his little nonsense sounds and fluffed out his feathers to rearrange them more neatly.

Remi sighed. "Well, I don't suppose you are the dream sender after all. You're only a bird. But you're in the dream, Waterfall. And in the other dream, you showed me the way to find out about Aderonke. I can't help feeling that you're doing something important in this dream, too. But all you seem to do, when you're in the dream at all, is fly to or from this old man's lap. I hope that doesn't mean I'm going to grow old on this island, with you flying back and forth! Does it mean it will be only the two of us forever?"

That night Remi's dream changed completely.

In his dream, Aderonke was sitting in the city apartment where Remi had seen her before. No one else was with her, and she seemed to be working very hard at something she was writing.

Then Remi heard a familiar voice sing, "Aderonke! Aderonke! Aderonke!"

Aderonke looked up, startled, as Waterfall flapped into the room and called her name. Instead of lighting on her shoulder, as he did with Remi, Waterfall came to rest on the table where Aderonke was working.

"Aderonke! Aderonke! Aderonke!" he sang again.

Aderonke smiled, and the bird sidled up to her, bobbing his head and trailing his beautiful tail across the table. He reached out one claw and tentatively placed it on her arm. Apparently, Aderonke wasn't frightened of Waterfall after he had quit flying and flapping around. She did not move her arm, and the parrot gently perched on it.

When Waterfall was comfortable, he broke into song:

> Aderonke! Aderonke! Aderonke!
> Without Aderonke, I would have drowned.
> Without Aderonke, I would have died of thirst.
> Without Aderonke, I would have succumbed.
> Without Aderonke, I would be long dead.
>
> You are my life to me, Aderonke.
> Never forget me, Aderonke!
> Always remember me, Aderonke!

Aderonke covered her mouth with her hand, and her eyes grew wide. The bird bobbed his head up and down, then cocked it to one side and looked at her out of one eye. He climbed up to her shoulder, where he settled down to nibble on her hair and mutter into her ear.

Likewise, Remi awoke with Waterfall muttering and chattering into his ear.

That night Remi dreamed again, but it was the old dream of darkness and the man with outstretched arms. For four more nights, Remi dreamed of the old man and not of Aderonke, and when Remi awoke on the fifth morning, Waterfall was gone.

Remi shook his head and wondered if he was still dreaming, but it was not so. The sun was streaming down between the leaves near his tree house, and he could hear the neighborhood birds chattering and singing in the branches.

"Waterfall!" he called. "Waterfall, where are you?" Remi scrambled down his ladder and looked around for his island companion.

"Waterfall!" he shouted. His voice set nearby birds to squawking, but Waterfall was nowhere to be seen.

Remi ran up the trail to the shrine, calling for the parrot. As he came out into the little clearing, he looked up and expected to find Waterfall circling above him.

Remi prayed distractedly at the shrine, begging for help in locating his only friend. "Oh, Aderonke, isn't it enough that I should have to live without you? How can I live without Waterfall, too?"

He ran back down the trail and out onto the beach. "Waterfall!" he called over and over. "Waterfall! Waterfall! Waterfall!"

Remi ran north along the beach until the shoreline turned. He strained his eyes against the sand and the sea and the sky, looking westward. There was not a sign of Waterfall. He turned and ran back south, all the way to where the shoreline again turned west, stopping once in a while to call the name of the bird with hands cupped around his mouth. When he could run no longer, he walked all the way to the marsh, where so many birds lived. He moved among them and hoped that Waterfall had come this way on some business.

It was a long, slow walk home.

He looked up at the sky periodically. Once in a while, he turned around and looked back where he had been. Perhaps he had missed Waterfall somehow? But most of the time, Remi walked with his head down, barely able to force himself to continue on his way home.

All that afternoon, Remi leaned against Aderonke's monument, looking out to sea. He did not call Waterfall again, and he did not look at the sky at all.

That night Remi dreamed twice. The first dream was of the old man in the darkness. But the second dream was exactly the same as the one he had dreamed five days ago—the dream of Waterfall making friends with Aderonke in the city apartment.

And in the morning, Remi awoke with Waterfall once again muttering and chattering into Remi's ear, pulling and tugging on Remi's hair. Remi wanted to leap on the bird, hug him to his chest, and never let go of him again, but he was afraid of startling Waterfall into flying away again. Remi lay perfectly still for the space of several heartbeats before he dared to speak.

"Waterfall, wherever in the world have you been?" he asked.

Waterfall cocked his head and hopped onto Remi's shoulder as Remi sat up.

"Do you know I spent all day yesterday looking for you? Do you know I was afraid to wake up today because you wouldn't be here? Do you know you're the only friend I have in the whole world, Waterfall?" Remi reached up carefully to stroke Waterfall's feathers, and the bird nibbled on his ear.

Waterfall sang a piece of the song he had learned:

Aderonke! Aderonke! Aderonke!
We will be together, Aderonke.
We will be together someday.
We will be together, Aderonke,
And I will love you forever.

Remi bit his lip and admitted, "How I wish that were true, Waterfall! How I wish that were true! Now that I know Aderonke is safe and well, I should be satisfied, but if she will have no other husband but me, I want to get to her so that we can be man and wife! But here I am on this island, and there she is in the city. She doesn't know where I am, and I can't get to where she is. What can I possibly do?"

Remi and Waterfall played together all that day, and Waterfall showed no sign of wanting to fly away. Remi lay in the sun with Waterfall prancing up and down his chest, and when Remi went to swim, the parrot watched him from Aderonke's monument. They had a nice chat with Aderonke and went hunting for pretty shells to take up to the shrine. They washed the salt and sand off the shells in the pool. Remi made flower garlands, while Waterfall picked them apart again with his beak. Remi was so happy to have Waterfall back again that he forgot about his unhappy separation from Aderonke...at least for a while.

When it was time to go to bed that night, Remi thought again about Waterfall's having gone off and left him for a day. He wondered if he should put the jess back on Waterfall's foot to make sure he doesn't fly away again. He decided that it probably wouldn't do any good because Waterfall had a very strong beak and was no longer a bumbling baby. He could snap that jess with his beak in an instant if he really wanted to go somewhere....

. . . Where would Waterfall want to go? Where *had* he gone? He could have flown to the other end of the island or even toward the center of the little rain forest, but why? If he wanted a mate, there were plenty of parrots nearby, and he had never shown any interest in any of them. Had he simply been hiding in a nearby tree, watching Remi run around frantically and calling his name? Surely not. Waterfall was far too affectionate and extremely attached to Remi. Could he have flown off the island? No, there was nowhere to go.

Remi was still pondering these questions when he fell asleep.

That night Remi slept fitfully. He awoke six times, each time from the dream of the old man. All six times, Remi felt around beside him to be sure Waterfall was still there. Finally, just before dawn, he fell into a deep sleep, and this time he dreamed of Aderonke.

She was sleeping in bed, but she seemed not to be sleeping well. She tossed about, occasionally flinging her arm over her eyes, and then she was very still. She put her hand over her mouth and turned her head slightly toward Remi. She did not open her eyes, but Remi got the impression that she was listening to something.

Remi listened, too, and what he heard was this:

Aderonke, Aderonke, Aderonke!
If Aderonke is not with me, I am lost.
If Aderonke is not with me, I have no family.
If Aderonke is not with me, I am barred from
   heaven.
If Aderonke is not with me, it does not matter
Whether I am alive or dead.

Why am I cast away at the prime of our love?
Why am I cast away when I am about to win
   you?
Why am I cast away by the wickedness of others?

*Why am I cast away to cry day and night?*
*Aderonke, Aderonke, Aderonke!*

The voice was not his, but Waterfall's. As it faded away, Aderonke seemed to relax. Her hand fell away from her mouth, which now had a little smile on it, and she began to sleep peacefully.

Then the scene of Remi's dream changed. It was the dream of the old man again; only something was different this time. The old man was not old. In fact, Remi was not at all surprised when he saw that the old man's arms looked very familiar, for they were his own. He could hear the voice chanting in the background as always, but this time he knew the voice—it, too, was his own. He saw Waterfall in this dream, and this time he felt the bird fly to his chest (even though it looked to him as if he were watching himself from some distance away) and disappear.

"Aderonke!" Remi cried. He sat up abruptly and knocked Waterfall off his chest, where the bird had settled down for a morning nap.

"Waterfall, I've got it! I know what to do! And it's you! It's been you all along!"

Remi looked hard at the parrot, who was preening his feathers after having been dumped on the floor of the tree house so suddenly. Waterfall ignored him.

Remi threw himself down on the floor with a thump and looked Waterfall straight in the face. He asked earnestly, "Waterfall, how much do you know about what's going on around here?"

The bird continued to preen his feathers.

*So,* Remi thought, *I've either got a very clever bird or he has no clue what he's doing. I really wish he could tell me how to go about this. I know what to do, but I don't know exactly how to do it. On the other hand, every bit of information that I've gotten so far I've gotten from that bird. And it looks as if I'm just going to have to be patient until he tells me the next step to take. . . .*

Remi had learned a great deal about patience on the island. He could either be patient and stay sane, or he could drive himself crazy with impatience. There was so little he could do to change his situation that he had learned to wait until the next step became clear, so Remi settled down to wait.

One thing Remi could do while he was waiting was try to recover the dream chant. He remembered only small snatches of it at first, but every time he dreamed the dream over the following days, he would remember a few more words. It was a difficult chant; the various parts of it seemed to twine in and out of one another, almost as if there was more than one person doing the chanting, but he was certain that it was only one voice in the dream.

Remi was convinced that this chant was one of great power, especially if it did what he thought it did. He considered writing it down so that he would not lose a single word of it, but he decided against this. He had never heard of a medicine man writing down any kind of chant, and he knew intuitively that writing it down would rob it of some of its power. He prayed every day that he would continue to have the dream long enough to hear and commit to memory the entire chant.

After three weeks, Remi had another dream about Aderonke.

In this dream, he was not himself, but Waterfall. He could feel himself flying, beating his strong wings against the wind. He flew over the city and came to rest on a veranda. He hopped to a windowsill, and there he saw Aderonke sleeping. But then something happened to him. He could feel himself growing smaller, and he could see the room growing larger. Aderonke herself took on tremendous proportions, as if he were only a mosquito.

Remi/Waterfall flew down to Aderonke's ear. Everything was dark, and he could hear Aderonke's blood beating like drums. Then Remi/Waterfall saw a light, and he realized it was the lamp that sat on the table in Nimi's sitting room. Aderonke was sitting at the table, writing. Aderonke looked up and was visibly startled as Remi/Waterfall flapped into the room calling her name. He settled on the table where Aderonke was working.

After the initial fear and surprise, Aderonke smiled. But as Remi/Waterfall began to move closer to her, bobbing his head and trailing his tail across the table, all grew dark again. He flew away from Aderonke's ear and out the window, growing as he flew. In a moment, Remi/Waterfall could smell the sea under him, and when he reached the tree house, he was very tired.

Remi slept late that morning, and when he awoke, he wondered why he felt so worn out. Then he remembered his dream, and he thought about it all day, trying to discern whether it had taught him anything new.

That night Remi dreamed of the old man again and of himself at the old man's side. Sometimes there were the two of them, and sometimes there seemed to be only one of them, but somehow Remi was always in the dream and so was the old man—as if sometimes they were two people and sometimes only one. Remi listened carefully to the chant and copied every gesture of the old man. By this time, Remi had an idea about who that old man might be, and Remi wanted to make sure he didn't miss even the tiniest detail of what he saw and heard in the dreams.

After two more months of watching Waterfall, of dreaming about the old man in the twilight, and of gathering the bits and pieces of the chant, Remi was sure he was ready.

# TEN

"Nimi, I need to talk to you about something," Aderonke said. They were sitting on the veranda, sipping a cool drink, watching Nimi's boys racing around in the sun.

"Of course, Aderonke! Are you having trouble in school?" Nimi was all sympathy.

"No, I've been doing better than I thought I would. Maybe that's because I don't have anything to do other than study. No, that's not what I need to talk to you about...." Aderonke bit her lower lip and frowned.

Nimi regarded her for a long moment and then asked, "Aderonke, is it a man?"

Aderonke flashed her a look, then smiled a rueful smile. "Well, now that you mention it, yes. It's Remi."

"Remi!" Nimi nearly dropped her drink. "Oh, you mean, you're feeling sad and depressed still?"

"No...no. Aunt Nimi, what does it mean if you dream about a dead person?"

"Ah! You've been dreaming of Remi?"

"Yes, only it's not like he's a ghost or anything. And they're not dreams about when he was alive. They're not even dreams about the things I wish we had been able to do—like dreams about the wedding we would have, the children we might have, or things like that. They're not that at all. I can't make any sense of it."

"Well, then, maybe you'd better explain this to me from the beginning. I've never set much store by dreams, but let's hear it."

Aderonke tucked her feet under her and began explaining, "The thing is I'm not even sure when this started. The strangest part of it is that when Remi first died, I didn't dream about him at all. Now isn't that strange? I teased him a lot, Nimi. I was really awful to him. But I wanted to marry Remi because he was the only one of my suitors who really seemed to see *me*. Do you know what I mean?"

Nimi nodded and said, "I certainly do. I know exactly what you mean! Some of them see your father's reputation, and some of them see the children you might have, and some of them see what other people will think of them if they marry you. That's one reason my parents had such a difficult time trying to find me a husband, and I wouldn't have married one even if they had found me one made of solid ivory! I married my husband because I knew that when he looked at me, he saw *me*." Nimi laughed. "So now he has a pretty wife and two fine sons, and everybody says how good I am at helping him in his career! But when we are together, he doesn't see these things. He sees the person I am, and I see the person he is, and we like being together."

"Exactly. Remi was a peasant; he was a nobody in the eyes of the world. But he saw me, and I saw him, and we liked being together." Aderonke stared into space for a time before she resumed her story. "Anyway, right after he died, I didn't dream of Remi at all. And this was strange because I prayed intensely that I would. I thought that maybe in a dream I could tell him I was sorry I had teased him so, and I also wanted to tell him I would never marry anyone else. I thought somehow if I dreamed of him, I could get into my own dream and tell him that, and I hoped that somehow he'd really hear me. You've no idea how terrible I felt."

"Yes, I do," Nimi said. "You blamed yourself for his death. It wasn't really your fault, you know. Truly, it wasn't. You couldn't read the future, and you didn't have any reason to distrust all those suitors who were saying nice things to you and bringing you presents. Even if you hadn't teased Remi, they would have acted the same way—and maybe even worse!"

"What do you mean?"

"I mean, you silly girl, that people who would kill Remi because they were jealous would not stop at killing your parents or even you. But who was to know they were so wicked?"

Aderonke's hand flew to her mouth. "Oh!" she cried. And then, her eyes growing wider, she yelled "Oh!" again. "That reminds me, Nimi. Isn't it funny that I did that with my hand in the dream?"

"Covered your mouth?"

"Yes. I guess I do that, don't I? I'd never noticed before."

"Start at the beginning, remember?"

"Oh, I'm sorry, Nimi. It's all so confusing! Let's see....The first thing I can remember is that I was running in some shallow water near a beach, and I was running toward the beach. And Remi was standing on the beach holding some flowers. There were lots of flowers all over the place on the sand. I remember it was a very white beach; the sand was so bright it hurt my eyes. But Remi was there, and I was running toward him, and he was holding up those flowers...." Aderonke's voice trailed off, and her lip quivered.

"Not a beach you knew? Not somewhere on the coast nearby?" Nimi asked.

"I don't think so. Just a plain beach. I can't remember anything else—no buildings or anything.

And Remi didn't say anything to me. He just held out those flowers. Then I remember another dream, but it was just a tiny portion of one, where Remi was talking to me just like he'd talk to me if he were sitting right here. He was holding a twisted and funny-shaped piece of wood, and he said the strangest thing. He said it was my dog!"

"That huge black animal of yours?" Nimi asked with a smile.

"Yes, that huge black animal of mine. Only it was just this little piece of wood. Isn't that strange?"

Nimi agreed that it was indeed strange. "How did you feel about this, Aderonke? Do you think Remi was being friendly? Or was he angry about the dog? I know that dog used to chase your suitors off!"

"Oh, no, Aunt Nimi. He was just as friendly as could be. It was as if he were giving me a little present or something. Do you know that Remi won over that dog in no time at all? And I think I remember him saying something about a 'secret place together,' but maybe it wasn't in that dream. I'm not sure."

"Is that all the dreams?"

"Oh, not at all! One time—don't laugh at me, Nimi—I dreamed that Remi gave me a cloak made of feathers. That's all I remember about that one, just the cloak slipping down over my shoulders and how it tickled! But I knew it had come from Remi. And then comes the really strange part. I began to dream this song. I know I hadn't heard it anywhere before, and the lyrics were addressed to me. I think one time I dreamed the whole song, and it was quite long, but I didn't really remember any of it when I woke up. Several times since then, I've dreamed part of it and not always the same part."

"Do you remember any of it now?" Nimi asked, tilting her head to one side.

"Oh, Nimi! It's like the parrot! That's exactly what the parrot does!"

"What parrot? I thought we were talking about a song," Nimi said, shaking her head.

"Oh, do be patient with me, Nimi!" Aderonke cried. "I had forgotten that part. Let me think....Well, the song begins with my name. It goes like this:

Aderonke, Aderonke, Aderonke!
If Aderonke is with me, this is my home.
If Aderonke is with me, she is my family.
If Aderonke is with me, she is my heaven.
If Aderonke is with me, it does not matter
Whether I am alive or dead.

"Nimi, do you think that was Remi's ghost speaking to me? Does he want me to die, too, so I can be with him?" Aderonke looked up at Nimi with such troubled eyes that Nimi nearly wept.

"No, Aderonke, I don't think so, but sometimes dreams do have important meanings for us if we search them out. Do you remember anymore of the song?"

"Only a line here and there, but I *know* I hear more of it in my dreams."

"How often do you dream like this?"

"At first it was only about once a month, but now it's nearly every night."

"What else is there in the dreams besides the song?" Nimi inquired.

"Oh, that's where the parrot comes in. The very first time I dreamed about this song was several months ago, I think. And it's strange because that was the most vivid of all the dreams. I can't remember any of the song that was in that dream, but it was the same song…just a different verse that I can't seem to remember no matter how hard I try, and somehow it seemed important. In my dream, I was in the sitting room studying. It was night, and I had the lamp on. I was writing something. This huge parrot—I mean, a really *big* parrot—flew in through the window. I've never seen a parrot that big. Its tail was longer than my arm, and it had the most beautiful blue-and-gold coloring you can possibly imagine. It flapped all over the room, and it scared me at first. I remember jumping up from my chair a little, but then the parrot settled down on the table and just looked at me. That's when it cocked its head the way you did a minute ago."

Nimi nodded.

"Then it sort of sidled over to me, and I was no longer afraid of it. That's when it sang the song. And it climbed up on my shoulder and nibbled my hair! I remember thinking what a nice bird it was, but then I woke up."

"And have you dreamed about the parrot again?"

"Yes, but not as vividly. Usually it's as if the parrot were singing to me, singing this song about me—only it's dark, and I can't really see it. And then sometimes the voice isn't the parrot's voice at all, but Remi's. But last night I dreamed again about the parrot flying into the sitting room, except it didn't stay as long. It settled down on the table and started to come over to me, but then it was gone. I don't think I woke up, yet the dream just stopped. And when I did wake up, I felt so lonely. What do you think it means, Aunt Nimi?"

Nimi shook her head. "I'm not sure, Aderonke, but I have a little idea."

"What is it?" Aderonke squealed. She was both glad to hear that her aunt might have solved the riddle and alarmed lest it be something terrible, though Aderonke had no idea what that "something terrible" might be.

"I'd rather not say just at the moment. I could be dreadfully wrong, and you wouldn't want an educated woman like me to say something stupid, would you?" Nimi smiled reassuringly, and Aderonke relaxed. "But I'll tell you what I think you should do about it."

"Wonderful!" Aderonke cried. "I was sure you would know what to do!"

"The first step is to remember as much of that song as you possibly can. Tonight when you go to bed, put a pencil and paper beside you, and when you wake from the dream, write down every word of the song that you can remember, even if it doesn't make sense. The more words we have, the better we'll be able to decide what the dream means."

For the next several weeks, Aderonke faithfully recorded anything she could remember of the song that appeared in her dreams. This is what she managed to collect over that time:

Why am I cast away at the prime of our love?
Why am I cast away when I am about to win you?
Why am I cast away by the wickedness of others?
Why am I cast away to cry day and night?

............ .

If I do not have Aderonke to love, I shall
never marry all my life.

. . . . . . . . . . . . .

Why do thugs try to kill the innocent?
Why does the sea carry away the lover?

. . . . . . . . . . . . .

Why is life so merciless?
Why do the evil suitors triumph?
Do they think I will forget my Aderonke?

. . . . . . . . . . . . .

I have no other life than Aderonke.
Aderonke has given me a purpose in life.
Aderonke has given me a mission in life.
Without Aderonke, I would have...

. . . . . . . . . . . . .

Here I have made a place for you.
Here I have made a home for you.
Here I have raised a monument to you.
Here I have decked a shrine for you.
Here I have declared...

. . . . . . . . . . . . .

We will be together, Aderonke,
And I will love you forever.


When Aderonke showed this collection of verses
to Nimi, her aunt looked very thoughtful. "Are you
sure these words are exact, Aderonke?"

"Yes, Aunt Nimi, I'm sure. I wrote down only exactly what I could remember, and if I wasn't sure, I just left it out. There were little pieces in between, but these are the only words I remember exactly, and I think this is the right order for everything to come in."

Nimi nodded. Finally she said, "Aderonke, I am going to write to your father."

What Nimi had to do now could be done only through her brother—Aderonke's father. After making several false starts on her letter, she figured out how to say what she had to say in a way that made sense but that wouldn't give anything away to anyone who happened to see the letter and had no business knowing about the matter at hand.

When Aderonke's father got the letter, he spoke to his wife about it. A few days later, Eli went to visit her sister, who lived in a nearby village. While she was visiting, of course, she stopped in to pay her respects to her father, who lived in the same village. Her father gave her a small gift and some careful instructions about using it.

Not long afterward, Aderonke's mother decided to visit the capital. She took along with her a great many gifts for her sister-in-law, Nimi, as she would be a guest in Nimi's house. Her neighbors congratulated her on this opportunity to stay in

Nimi's fine apartment and meet people who were important in the government. And they sent their congratulations to Nimi, who was soon to have another child. Everyone agreed that Eli was kind and generous to go take care of her little nephews at this time when her own poor daughter was so recently deceased.

On this trip, Eli brought with her—in a tiny bag hung on a cord around her neck—the present her father had given her when she had visited him.

Aderonke was overjoyed to see her mother again. There was much gossiping, and Aderonke took Eli to visit the university. Eli got along famously with Nimi's husband and was somewhat awed by the important guests Nimi entertained. The twins enjoyed having their aunt visit with them, as most of the family lived in villages and did not come to the city often. In short, it was a very enjoyable visit for all involved.

Eli stayed two months, during which time Nimi became the mother of another little boy and Aderonke applied herself earnestly to study. Then Eli returned home, and her neighbors noticed that both she and her husband seemed happier now. Perhaps the visit had done her some good, and she had enjoyed having someone to fuss over.

Shortly after this, Aderonke's dreams became much clearer. Almost every night she dreamed that the blue-and-gold parrot flew into the sitting room, sat on the table, and sang to her a part of the song that began with her name. In the morning, Aderonke awoke and wrote down what the parrot had sung.

In about two weeks, Aderonke was certain she had the entire song. She showed the lyrics to Nimi, who simply said, "I thought so."

"What do you mean? What did you think, Aunt Nimi?"

"Why, that Remi is alive, of course!"

"Alive! Oh, Aunt Nimi, how can you say that? Do you want me to cry and tear my hair out by the roots? You know those thugs killed him!" Aderonke burst into tears.

"Hush! Hush, Aderonke!" Nimi said crossly. "Now you just hush! I wouldn't say such a thing unless I was certain. I didn't tell you all this time, but I was just about certain when you first told me about the dreams. You know that I wrote to your father, right?"

"Yes," Aderonke said between sniffles.

"He sent your mother to visit your grandfather, and your grandfather gave her something to bring to your home. That little 'something' is under your bed, and now your dreams are a lot clearer, aren't they?"

"Why, yes! But I thought you didn't put much stock in such things, Aunt Nimi!"

"Well, that's what you thought! There's a place for everything, Aderonke. There's a time to use your government connections to get a helicopter, and there's a time to ask for help from your medicine man grandfather!"

"Oh!" That was all Aderonke could say.

"Now we have the whole song. I admit that if you think of it as something from the land of the dead, it sort of makes sense. But if you think of it as coming from a living person who is in a far-off place, it makes a lot more sense. Listen to this part, for instance:

Without Aderonke, I would have drowned.
Without Aderonke, I would have died of thirst.
Without Aderonke, I would have succumbed.
Without Aderonke, I would be long dead.

"Do you hear that? It doesn't make sense if Remi is dead!"

Aderonke covered her mouth with her hand as tears streamed down her face. Overcome with emotion, she simply nodded in complete agreement.

"Now what we have to do," Nimi continued, "is figure out what we can do about this. If Remi is alive, where is he? He is certainly not anywhere around your home village. I think he's where you saw him in your first dream: on a deserted beach somewhere."

"But why doesn't he just come home?" Aderonke wailed.

"Maybe he can't get home," Nimi suggested.

"Why not? He can walk if he doesn't have money."

"What if he's not where he can walk?"

"Where could that be?"

"Well, what if he's across the ocean?"

"Across the ocean! How in the world could he get across the ocean?"

"I don't know! Those thugs tried to drown him, didn't they? Maybe he caught a ride on a fishing boat."

"Then why didn't he just come home after the fishing boat stopped in port?"

"Maybe it sank. I don't know." Nimi furrowed her brow and added, "I wonder how we can find out where that beach is."

"Maybe we should ask grandfather."

"Maybe we should," Nimi said. "Maybe we should."

# ELEVEN

Remi decided to wait until the dark of the moon, which somehow seemed the right time to do the thing he had in mind. Meanwhile, he practiced the dream chant, but he always did so in broad daylight and very quietly, after having put a little distance between himself and Waterfall.

When the dark of the moon arrived, Remi was ready. He watched the stars wheeling in the sky until he was sure it was very late at night. Then he sat on the beach, holding Waterfall in his lap and stroking his feathers. Remi stared out to sea in the direction of home—and Aderonke.

After another long time, Remi began to sing. He held his arms out in front of him and was not surprised when his eyes seemed to close of their own volition.

It was not difficult to remember the chant. He had practiced and practiced over the last few days, but it was not the practicing that helped him remember it. Rather, the song seemed to rise up from somewhere deep inside him, as if he had never learned it from anyone. No one but Remi knew the exact words of that special dream song.

Remi sang of distances and of Aderonke sleeping. He sang of islands and his own despair. He sang of visions and dreams and prayers. He sang of faithfulness to his promised bride and her faithfulness to him. He sang of being together. But most of all, he sang of one thing: his location.

"Here I am!" sang his song. "Here I am!"

Remi sang for over an hour, although he did not know it. When he stopped singing, his arms fell to his sides. They were numb.

When Remi opened his eyes, Waterfall was gone. He had neither heard the parrot fly away nor felt him leave his lap, but Remi knew where he had gone.

Remi waited until the stars wheeled farther in their courses. Then he lifted his arms again and began to sing once more.

Again Remi sang of distances, of his own loneliness, of Aderonke—his most precious treasure. And again he sang, "Here I am!"

Remi could not keep his eyes open, and he did not see or feel Waterfall's return. But when the sun came up, Remi's song ended, and Waterfall was nestled in his lap.

Remi slept most of that day, and Waterfall slept perched on his arm. And this was the pattern for the next three days and nights. During the night, he chanted with his arms outstretched and his eyes closed. And during the day, he slept…dreamless.

When these four days were over, Remi felt strange. When he looked at the sky, he saw things he had not noticed before. When he looked at the ground, it was as if he could see through the earth and out the other side. He could feel everything moving under his feet, and it gave him vertigo. Waterfall's silly mutterings and chattering revealed information he had not previously known, and Remi found that the fishes spoke a language of their own. Even the grasses spoke to him, and he listened for messages in the wind. Sometimes it seemed to him as if he could see everything around him moving more slowly than he normally could. For example, when Waterfall flapped and fluffed out his feathers, Remi was able to watch each little bit of feather fan out slowly, straighten, and fold in like a flower. He spent long hours watching the waves roll in and the grains of sand shift on the beach.

At first, these feelings of strangeness lasted only a few minutes. Then Remi would shake his head, laugh at himself, and go about some ordinary task. But over the following days and weeks, the times of sensory strangeness grew lengthier, and Remi had a harder time shaking himself out of them. Before the next dark of the moon arrived, Remi gradually got used to the strangeness, walking in it most of his waking hours.

And at night, Remi no longer dreamed. It was as if he now walked in a dream all the time, seeing and hearing things that he had never before been able to see or hear. Time and distance were distorted. Shapes changed before his eyes. Only Waterfall was constant—always there, always the right size and shape and color.

By the next dark of the moon, Remi knew what had taken root in him, and he was glad. But even his gladness was different—not the whooping, jolly sort of joy he had been accustomed to feeling, but a fierceness, a wildness somewhere in his belly.

For four nights at the dark of the moon, Remi sang again. The chant was so strong this time that it was as if he could feel himself going out of himself and into Waterfall. He could feel himself flying, and he knew where he was going. The fierce, wild joy sprang up in him as he flew, and the chant beat in his blood: "Here I am!"

After these four days and nights, Remi slept a whole day and night, and when he awoke, he was ravenously hungry. He did almost nothing but eat for a whole day, and Waterfall seemed as hungry as he was. He was so disoriented that he could hardly walk without stumbling. He fell down, as if intoxicated. But his hunger drove him to keep moving about, looking for more food.

In a few days, Remi recovered both his strength and his ability to tell up from down. But the strangeness now remained with him all the time. He would have to stop and think about having to do the most ordinary activities, or he might go an entire day without eating, but most of the time he seemed to be walking in a dream world, even though he could feel the sand under his feet.

Remi no longer talked to the monument of Aderonke. Sometimes he went out to the barrier and sat beside the cairn, rigid as stone himself, staring out to sea. But he did not speak.

The third month, Remi repeated his chanting at the dark of the moon. He could feel his own power—a power that seemed to come from the depth of the earth and the depth of the sea and to fall down from heaven itself—far stronger than before. He had no memory of what happened that time, on any of the four nights.

Remi did not wake until nightfall two days afterward. He was in the tree house, and Waterfall was sitting on the branch Remi had brought for him to perch on. Remi could feel the tree house lurch and sway under him, as if there was a storm, but he heard no wind. Waterfall cocked his head and looked at Remi from one eye. He preened two of his tailfeathers and looked at Remi again.

"You've got to control this," Waterfall said.

Remi tried to focus his eyes. *Was that Waterfall that spoke? How could Waterfall think with the floor swaying and bucking as it was?* Remi shook his head. The sides of the tree house seemed to melt and run down themselves, first green and then other colors, too—colors Remi had not imagined, let alone seen, at any time in his life. Remi blinked, and the floor lurched so badly that he shut his eyes and desperately grabbed for one of the upright supports of the tree house to keep from sliding right out the side.

As soon as he shut his eyes, the vertigo stopped. He wasn't sliding at all. True, he could feel the tree growing and changing under him. He could feel its roots reaching down into the earth, its leaves stretching for the sun. He could feel the insects that made their homes in the tree and in the earth nearby.

He could feel the earth itself down, down....Remi stopped thinking at all, feeling dizzier than ever.

"You've got to control this," Waterfall repeated.

Remi opened his eyes abruptly. Everything around him was steady, although he could feel the life of the tree and the ground.

"What did you say, Waterfall?"

"You've got to control this," the parrot said.

Remi could not be surprised. He knew that Waterfall spoke. All creatures spoke...if you could only understand their language. But Waterfall was *telling* him something, not merely talking. Waterfall knew more about Remi's own condition than Remi himself did.

Be that as it may, Remi was too hungry to try to figure out what Waterfall was telling him. He spent the next hour stumbling around in the dark, gathering fruit. After he and the parrot had eaten as much as they could hold, Remi fell asleep, and he stayed asleep until after sunrise.

Happily, Remi awoke with a clear head. He could feel the life of the earth around him, but things seemed to have a more normal appearance. He swam out to the barrier reef and sat with Waterfall most of the day, but he prepared an especially large dinner that evening. He knew the giddiness would be worse if he forgot to eat.

He thought most of the day about what Waterfall had said. Most of what Remi understood of the parrot's mutterings and chattering was bird talk: Waterfall's own thoughts interspersed with a few words from some song or another that Remi had taught him. Waterfall did not speak man talk except to repeat the words of the songs. But this was man talk. Remi was sure of it. Waterfall had said quite plainly, "You've got to control this."

Remi knew what he had to control. His own mind was now in touch with so many elements around him that all these forces beat upon him at once. They distorted his perceptions while enabling him to perceive things he had not previously known were there. He must learn to control those perceptions, or they would kill him. He would be driven completely insane and eventually do something fatal like walk off a high tree branch.

After thinking about it a while, Remi decided that the first thing he needed to do was maintain his normal daily routine. He would check the sun often and remember to go swimming, to eat well and regularly, and to spend some time each day doing something simple like weaving a basket or mending a net. It would probably be best for him not to sit out in the sun on the barrier to do his thinking, as the heat and the glare might make matters worse.

Taking his own advice, Remi swam back to the beach and went with Waterfall up to Aderonke's shrine. Here was a quiet and cool thinking place. This might be a good place to begin to gain some control over his own perceptions. He lay in the grass and just felt the grass and listened to the earth underneath him, trying to shut out the sky and the insects and the birds and the sea.

For the next two weeks, Remi settled into a regular routine. When he awoke, he went up to the shrine and prayed for guidance, for help in controlling the forces that beat upon him from without and within. Then he went swimming for his breakfast. He forced himself to cook fish and yams every morning. After breakfast, he went for a long, slow walk, always determining ahead of time exactly how far he would go. During these walks, he concentrated on allowing only some of his new perceptions into his mind. He focused on what the sand was doing or on the messages of the grasses that grew near the beach or on the patterns of breeze in the air. When he reached his predetermined destination, he turned around to walk back, this time deliberately trying to keep in touch with the "normal" physical world as he had known it, blocking out the new perceptions entirely. In this, he was not very successful, but at least he managed to avoid falling on his face or walking into the ocean.

After his walk, Remi returned to the shrine again to think, taking with him the tools for completing some simple task. Part of the time he practiced controlling his perceptions and listening to the messages around him, and part of the time he concentrated only on doing something with his hands. When the sun got close to the top of the trees on the western side of the clearing above the waterfall, Remi picked up his handiwork and went back down to the beach to cook his supper.

Remi went to sleep early every day, striving to build his strength for the next dark of the moon. Before he went to sleep, he allowed himself to think over the lessons he had learned during the day, but he never thought so deeply that he got dizzy and sick. He usually felt disoriented when he awoke in the morning, but he never again experienced the terrible vertigo and sickness that had attacked him that first evening.

Remi carefully followed this new routine for the entire month, and when he approached the next dark of the moon, he felt a great deal stronger than he ever had before. He was now used to walking in his dreamworld and seldom had trouble keeping his balance or realizing where he was. But if he looked, he could see far into the earth beneath his feet, and even without listening too intently, he could hear the voices in the sea.

Remi had settled down into a new kind of calm. His perceptions no longer whirled around him, battering him from every side. Somehow Remi had accomplished what Waterfall had urgently instructed him to do.

He had occasionally wondered how Waterfall could have spoken to him in this way. Remi had an idea about this, but he could not be certain until he had a chance to speak with someone who knew more about such things than he did. Waterfall never repeated his remark after that evening, and he never again spoke in man talk.

On that dark of the moon, everything went as Remi hoped it would. He remembered what had happened, as if he had been watching himself from some distance away but yet feeling everything himself. When the four days were over, he slept a full day and night. He awoke feeling only a little dizzy and extremely hungry. But better than any food was the knowledge that he had won a great victory over himself and over the forces within and around him. And he was certain that he had succeeded at what he set out to do.

Remi kept up his regular daily routine after this, but he lit the signal fire once again and left it burning brightly every night. And during the day, he damped it down with wet wood and leaves to produce a great deal of smoke.

He also began to work on a new song that he knew he would soon have the opportunity to sing.

# TWELVE

Once again, Nimi wrote to her brother, and once again, Eli went to visit her sister. Eli stayed in the neighboring village for two weeks, and much of this time was spent in the house of her father, the medicine man.

Eli did not carry any gifts back with her this time—at least not any gifts that could be seen by the curious. But she had learned something very precious, and she brought that learning back with her. She did not share it with anyone, not even her husband, although late at night they whispered together when everyone else in the village was asleep.

Two weeks later, Eli decided that she would like to visit her sister-in-law again, and this visit was made much easier because her husband had business to take care of in the city. He professed a desire to see his nephews while he was on his business trip, so he and his wife made plans to stay at Nimi's house.

Because Eli's husband had often had such business in the city, the neighbors were not particularly surprised when the couple extended their stay. Business can sometimes be complicated, and as a result, Nimi's brother and sister-in-law stayed with her for over four months.

After Nimi and her husband had finished doing all the polite things one does when relatives come for a prolonged visit, Eli had an opportunity to talk privately with Nimi and Aderonke.

"I think I have everything you will need," she said. "Well, almost everything. Can your husband get a good large map for us?"

I think so," Nimi answered. "What sort of map do you need?"

"Father said it must be a map that shows all the west coast and all the South Atlantic Ocean and the east coast of South America."

"Whoever would make a map of the ocean? There aren't any towns or roads or mountains!" Aderonke blurted out.

"I believe the navy would have such maps," Nimi said. "I'm sure of it. They have to know about things like currents and the depth of the water near coast-lines and where—because they have to know where all the islands are!" Brimming over with optimism, Nimi smiled.

"You mean we can find where Remi is on a map because he has to be on an island somewhere in the ocean!" Aderonke exclaimed.

"Or he's possibly on the seacoast somewhere where there aren't any other people," Eli said.

"But how can we possibly find Remi in all that ocean?" Aderonke asked. "There must be thousands of islands out there…and thousands of miles of coastline! If we had all the money in the world, we couldn't hire someone to look at every island and every mile of beach! Why, it would take more than a lifetime, anyway!"

"It would if we had to hire someone to search all the islands and all the beaches," Eli said, "but we can do the searching ourselves. Or rather, you can do it, Aderonke."

"But how? I don't have a boat!"

"No, of course not. Father has shown me how to do it, and I will show you. I think we should get the map first, and then the rest of it might make more sense."

Nimi's husband was used to the odd requests made of him by his independent-minded wife, and in fact, he was pleased to comply with them. It gave him a certain feeling of distinction—how many wives were as clever as his? He spoke to some of his friends in various government offices, and after about ten days, Nimi had her map.

Or maps, rather. The South Atlantic Ocean is very big indeed, and the naval charts were large in scale. Aderonke found that if she spread them out on her floor, she could open only a few of them at a time. The search was likely to be a long one.

After the women talked this situation over, they decided that they should use several maps at once, with their edges fitted together to show one area of the ocean and coast. They would concentrate only on that section of the ocean, then roll those charts up and begin on another section.

While they had been waiting for the maps to arrive, Eli had been teaching Aderonke everything her father had told her. This proved to be quite complex. Amn other things Aderonke had to learn a long and difficult chant, which would have to be done perfectly every single night.

They also went to the market to buy a parrot.

Aderonke's grandfather had been adamant about this. He told Eli that he himself could call a parrot for this purpose, but it would be the wrong parrot. Aderonke must find it herself, and it must be the bird that felt "right" to her. Only she would know exactly which bird this was, and it did not matter if she took several months to find it, . The important thing was finding the right one.

The first day they went parrot shopping, they went to the market where all kinds of animals and birds were sold, along with produce, fruit, and other items from the countryside. Aderonke felt most comfortable in this market, and Eli had always come here when she had lived in the city.

Because this was the capital, the market was quite large. Some of the vendors had booths, but some of them simply spread out their wares on the ground. It seemed to Aderonke as if everyone for miles around had come to buy or to sell or even to barter. She usually liked to hear the many languages spoken, admire the jewelry crafted by people from some district other than her own, and watch the Europeans haggling for a good price. But this time she simply wished all the customers would go away so that she could look and listen for her special parrot.

A very disappointed Aderonke returned, with her very tired mother and aunt, after a long day at the market. Aderonke thought she surely must have walked back and forth a dozen times to every vendor. She had seen plenty of birds, many of them parrots. There were the little gray ones that were supposed to be the best talkers, but they looked at her with hostile eyes, and she could not bear even to touch one of them. There were little ones that hung by their feet when they slept, but Aderonke did not want anything at all like a bat. There were bright green lovebirds, but all of them were in pairs, and Aderonke knew she had to get only one.

Aderonke had been attracted to a lovely little parrot from India, with a bright magenta head and a long blue-and-yellow tail, but when Aderonke tried to talk to the bird, it moved away from her on its perch. No matter how pretty it looked, this was clearly not the right parrot.

That night Aderonke spoke to her uncle about the problem of finding just the right parrot.

"Uncle Ade," she said, "I must find exactly the right parrot, and I had terrible luck at the market today. What can I do?"

"You certainly are particular!" her uncle answered. "Whatever do you want a parrot for?"

"Um...I am lonely here without my parents, Ade. You know I love Aunt Nimi and the boys, but I have always been close to my parents. It is hard being away from them. I thought that if I found just the right parrot, I might teach it to say some of the things my parents often say to me. And if it hears them say things, it will mimic them. So if I find a good parrot while they are still here visiting, it will talk like them after they leave. Do you think that's silly?" Aderonke gave her uncle her most charming and wide-eyed look.

"Why, um...hmm...of course not, Aderonke! It's really quite clever of you to think of such a thing.

Well, of course, you have to find just the right parrot. I've heard that the gray ones are the best talkers."

"Yes, I know. I saw several of them today at the market. Some had the most beautiful red tails, and others had already learned to talk a little. But they all looked at me as if they hated me! I don't think I'd be very happy having some bird speak to me—especially in my parents' voices—and looking at me like that!"

"I see your point. Let me think....There's an exotic-animal market run by the government, but you're supposed to be a recognized dealer even to go in there." Ade wrinkled up his forehead.

"Do you know any dealers?" Aderonke asked.

"No...no, I don't. Let me ask around and see if I know someone who knows a dealer. You know, these people have special import and export licenses, and they mostly sell to zoos and similar institutions. A few of the animals go to pet shops overseas. But what you'd see there would be about the same as what you saw today, I'm afraid."

"Don't they bring any exotic animals in?"

"Yes, they do, but usually those have already been ordered by someone here. Some government official or someone with a lot of money. One of the most important men in my bureau has a kangaroo! Can you believe that?"

"A kangaroo? Isn't that from Australia?"

"It sure is. And they're only supposed to go to zoos, but this person has one. I don't know what in the world he does with it, but it hops around in his courtyard whenever he has guests! I suppose if he can get a kangaroo, then we can find you your parrot!" Ade smiled and added, "Don't fret, Aderonke. I'll ask around and see what I can find out."

Aderonke tried hard to contain her impatience for the next several days while her uncle "asked around." But she was hopeful when he came home from work one evening with a glint in his eye.

"Aderonke," he said, "I think we've found it!"

"What? The parrot?"

"I think so. It isn't just one parrot, so I think you may be able to pick out the right one. Let me tell you about it." Ade sat down, his two big boys crowding around him and hopping from foot to foot as they tried to get his attention. "Do you remember the man with the kangaroo that I told you about?"

Aderonke nodded.

"Well, he told me about a friend of his who has birds—not just a pair or even only a few. He's got hundreds of them! He fancies parrots of all kinds and imports them from all over the world. He's got Amazon parrots and cockatoos and parakeets and macaws and I don't know what else. He keeps them in aviaries, or big cages that have little trees growing in them for the birds to perch on. Of course, every once in a while, they raise families of young parrots. And that means his aviaries get too full, and he has to get rid of some of the extra birds. Mostly he exports—not to pet shops and zoos, but exclusively to other bird fanciers. He's got a whole network of bird fanciers all over the world, and they sell birds to one another. And then sometimes he gives them away as gifts. Of course, anyone who gets one of them has to become a bird fancier, too! You wouldn't believe how many government officials and bankers and other important people in this country have exotic birds!"

Aderonke giggled.

"But here's the good news....The man I spoke to has introduced me to this bird fancier. I explained to him that I have a lovely niece who is looking for exactly the right parrot, and he invited us to his home to look at his birds. I rather think you will find what you want."

"To his home! Oh!" Aderonke's hand flew to her mouth, and her eyes grew wide. "Oh!" she repeated.

Aderonke had never seen such a home in her life. She knew her father was a wealthy man, but he was not nearly this wealthy. She knew her uncle was an important man in government—and becoming more important every day—but he was not nearly this important.

There were servants. Aderonke tried to count them, but she lost track. There was a high wall around the house, and she was invited into two courtyards, The house was so large, Aderonke was certain that there must be other courtyards as well. The courtyards were filled with lush gardens with flowering trees. And high above each courtyard was a vaulted wire mesh roof.

When she first walked into the courtyard, Aderonke was overwhelmed with the chatter and whistle and screech and song of what must have been four hundred birds. She didn't see any of them at first, but she soon discovered that some of the "flowers" on the trees weren't flowers at all. And some of the "leaves" were really birds with bright green plumage.

She exclaimed in delight.

"I see you like my little friends," her host said. He whistled a tune, and a perky cockatiel flew down from a tree to perch on his head. He reached up and put the bird on his finger, whistling and clucking to it as he did so. "This is Tangerine. You see the little orange circles on his cheeks? Most of these birds are fairly wild, but Tangerine is very much a pet. He spends most of his time in the sitting room instead of out here with the others."

"Hello there!" Tangerine said.

"Why, hello there, Tangerine," Aderonke answered. "May I hold him?"

"Of course. He's quite friendly."

Gingerly, Aderonke took Tangerine on her finger. The bird cocked his head and looked at her out of one eye.

*That's just what the bird in my dream did,* Aderonke thought. *Do they all do that?*

"Tell me," she said, "do they all cock their heads like that?"

"Yes," her host answered, "I think they can see you better if they just look out of one eye. If they look out of both eyes, it's more for distance vision. That way they can see all around them when they're flying."

"I see," Aderonke said, handing Tangerine back to her host. "May I look around?"

"By all means. And feel free to ask any questions. I like nothing better than to talk about my little friends."

When Aderonke and her uncle went home that evening, they took with them a large carrying cage, enough food to feed an army of parrots for months, and a headful of instructions on caring for a parrot. In the cage was a very young red macaw. Aderonke's host had refused to sell the bird, insisting on making it a gift.

The next few days were spent taming the baby macaw. Because the baby preferred to snuggle up to Aderonke at every opportunity, apparently having adopted her as its mother, taming was no trouble at all. Aderonke trained the bird to stay on a perch, and it showed absolutely no inclination to fly out the window. It was not long before she and the bird were inseparable. For reasons she could not explain to herself, Aderonke named the macaw Paradise.

Meanwhile, Aderonke practiced her chant. She was careful to follow her grandfather's instructions exactly, never practicing the chant around anyone other than her mother, but always in daylight and always around the baby parrot. She finally felt ready, and she waited anxiously for the dark of the moon.

Aderonke waited until midnight. Everyone in the house was asleep, and she was alone in her own room. She opened the window wide and sat on the mat, holding Paradise in her lap. She took several deep breaths to calm herself—she mustn't make a single mistake!—and began to sing very softly. There was a strength behind the softness that made her voice seem to swell—but only to the walls, no farther. Every crevice of the room was filled with Aderonke's song, but a person standing on the street outside could not have heard a word of it.

Aderonke sang for a long time. The chant was a secret, and she never told anyone the words, but she sang of her loneliness, of her joy at knowing

Remi was alive and safe, of her faithfulness to him, of her desire to bear his children and his alone, of the long months she had spent at the university studying topics she really did not care about. But most of all, her song asked these questions: "Where are you? Where can I find you?"

When the song was finished, Aderonke did not open her eyes. She held Paradise close to her and settled down to sleep. If she dreamed that night, she did not remember it in the morning.

Aderonke woke to bright sunshine. Instead of going to greet the other members of her family, she set Paradise on her arm and spread out the first four of the maps. For a long time, she sat cross-legged on the floor, studying them, letting her mind drift. She imagined the water and sand and clouds. She felt as if she were looking down from a great height—like a bird in flight.

After a while, Aderonke sighed, rolled up the charts, and went to say good morning to her aunt and uncle.

"You look tired, Aderonke," Nimi said at breakfast. "Was it a difficult night?"

"No, not really," Aderonke answered. "The things I had to do weren't so difficult, but I don't think I'm having much luck yet."

"What did you have to do, Aderonke?" her uncle asked innocently.

"Oh, just some work," she answered vaguely.

Her uncle smiled indulgently and then gently cautioned, "Well, you mustn't work too hard, Aderonke. I'm sure you'll do very well at the university without wearing out your pretty head all night."

Aderonke's uncle was very modern, and it wasn't wise to talk about such matters in front of people who didn't understand them—so she didn't correct his assumptions.

"Thank you, Uncle Ade," she said. "I hope I will."

Aderonke was hardly able to think about anything all day except for what she was going to do that night. She began to have doubts. *I had no luck the first time. Will my second try be any better? Am I just being foolish? What if Remi is dead after all?* She tried hard to push such thoughts out of her mind, and she practiced her chant over and over in her head to make certain it was perfect.

That night Aderonke tried again. The chant came more easily, and she felt a little more confident this time. But the next morning when she looked at the charts, she was disappointed again.

Eli and Nimi saw Aderonke's disappointment but did not know how to comfort her.

The third night, Aderonke didn't think she could possibly finish the chant correctly. There seemed to be a dozen mosquitoes in the room, all of them determined to bite her, but she dared not open her eyes or move to slap them away. But somehow she managed, and when she went to bed, she was worn out.

When she looked at the charts the next morning, Aderonke seemed to feel a sort of pull, not to the charts themselves but to an area that would have been west of one of them. But Aderonke could not make much sense out of the charts herself, and she could not decide which of the other maps would be the one to the west of the map she was looking at. Nevertheless, she felt somewhat heartened. She was getting some kind of response, and she had hope that she would indeed find Remi if only she was persistent enough.

Aderonke was extremely tired from her efforts, however, and when she began her chant on the fourth night, she had a hard time remembering the words. When she finished, she was not entirely certain that she had done it correctly, and in the morning, the maps told her nothing at all.

Nimi and Eli did their best to console Aderonke, reminding her that her grandfather had expected the search to take many months. While she waited for the dark of the moon to arrive again, Aderonke ate heartily, caught up on her schoolwork, and enjoyed training her pet parrot.

Meanwhile, Aderonke asked her uncle if he could help her read the naval charts. She was always vague about what exactly she was looking for, but Ade was happy to try to please his niece, especially since he had no daughter of his own. After a few days, Aderonke had a fairly good idea which of the charts she wanted to try next time.

The month dragged by for Aderonke, but the day finally came to try again. She practiced her chant and would have forgotten to eat dinner had her mother not reminded her.

The next morning, she was sure she felt something, but she wasn't sure what.

"Nimi," she asked her aunt after breakfast, "do you think I should try these same charts again? I don't know what to think."

"I would if I were you," Nimi answered. "And you might try all those maps that would be next to these if they were all laid out in order."

"Let's see," Aderonke said, counting on her fingers, "that would be twelve more....I couldn't finish them all if I did these again. Honestly, Aunt Nimi, I don't know what to do."

"I think you should take it slow," Nimi said. "It would be better to progress slowly and be certain, even if it does take several months."

During the third month, Aderonke felt a little more sure of herself and of the direction in which she should look. By the fourth month, she was almost certain which map would show the area where she might find Remi. She took a chance and concentrated on that one alone.

On the fourth morning of the fourth month, Aderonke came to breakfast wreathed in smiles.

# THIRTEEN

It was almost sunset, and Remi was building up his signal fire on the beach. He had just shared a rather large dinner with Waterfall and was thinking of going to bed soon. At the moment, the flames were roaring. For some reason, Waterfall was screeching a great deal. Remi enjoyed Waterfall's chattering, muttering, and singing. He also thought Waterfall's meaningless snatches of speech were pleasantly companionable. But the parrot's screech was earsplitting. As a result, Remi did not hear the boat approaching the reef.

When he finally turned around to bid good night to Aderonke's monument, Remi felt that once again he had lost control of his perceptions. He was dreaming while wide awake!

It was certainly just like the dream he had had the day he washed up on the coral reef, but this time he could see far more detail. Just beyond the barrier there was a small motorboat. Its white sides were bathed in the colors of the sunset and featured some sort of government insignia on it.... Remi could now see that it was flying the flag of his own nation. There were four people standing by the railing, waving at him. About a hundred yards away, a man in a naval uniform was beaching a little boat. Remi could not remember seeing any of these things in his previous dream.

But the most important part of his other dream was there: Aderonke running toward him, splashing through the little waves at the edge of the beach.

Remi shook his head, closed his eyes, and tried to exert control. *Think about breathing,* he told himself. *Breathe in, breathe out. Breathe in, breathe out....*

At that moment, Remi was nearly knocked to the ground as something hit his chest and wound itself tightly around him.

Waterfall squawked the following:

Aderonke! Aderonke! Aderonke!
We will be together, Aderonke.
We will be together someday.
Aderonke, Aderonke, Aderonke!

"Remi! Oh, Remi! It's really you! You're really here! Remi, I'm so glad I found you!"

Remi opened his eyes in astonishment. Aderonke was in his arms, real and warm. She was very much not a dream, not a vision, not a misperception of any kind at all. She was laughing and crying and calling his name over and over, while Waterfall strutted about on the sand, whistling and squawking and occasionally giving one of his earsplitting shrieks.

But even in this first shock of discovery, Remi felt a new strangeness in himself and in Aderonke. He was no longer the peasant boy hopelessly attempting to win the rich man's beautiful daughter. She was no longer the silly, spoiled child playing games with the suitors who brought her gifts. Both of them had suffered much, and both had learned from their suffering. Remi could feel in himself the power that had reached out to call Aderonke to him, and he could feel in Aderonke the resolute maturity that had overcome great difficulties to answer his summons.

He held her for a long time, filled with joy.

Remi was taken out to the motorboat that evening. He was greeted by Aderonke's parents, Nimi, and an older man in an elaborate naval uniform. During the course of a long evening's conversation, Remi learned that the uniformed man was not only in charge of the coastal rescue and survey force—he was also a fancier of exotic birds. This man was much taken with Waterfall, but the parrot would have nothing to do with anyone other than Remi— and Aderonke.

They drank palm wine in celebration of Remi's rescue, and they discussed at length how it came about. Several theories were proposed concerning how Remi and Aderonke could have begun to reach each other through their dreams.

That night Remi and the others slept on the boat, but they did not start home until the next day. He wanted to show Aderonke the shrine and speak to her privately about what had happened to him on the island.

He took her for a swim in the reef after breakfast, and Aderonke marveled at the underwater land with its bright fishes and fantastic corals. They walked up the beach together, and Aderonke picked up a few unusual shells to take home with her. As they climbed up into the tree house, Aderonke admired Remi's handiwork with the baskets, mats, and other items he had made and adapted for his own use. When they walked through the rain forest, Aderonke picked an armful of fragrant flowers of kinds she had never seen before.

Then Remi took Aderonke up to the shrine.

They sat on the black rock at the edge of the pool, with their feet in the water. The spray from the waterfall misted their faces. Remi showed Aderonke all the objects he had put on the ledge behind the waterfall.

"There it is!" Aderonke exclaimed.

"What?"

"The little dog—the piece of wood over there! I saw it in my dream. You were handing it to me and saying it was my dog, or I thought it was my dog. I can't remember exactly….Oh, Remi, everything is so lovely! It breaks my heart to have to leave here. Do you think we should leave these things here, or do you want to take them with us?"

"I hadn't thought about it….You know, these things were meant for you. What would you like to do? If you want to keep them, we can bring them along. Or you can leave them here if you want to. This will always be a special place to us—no matter where we are—because of what has happened here. You decide."

Aderonke thought a long time, staring past the falling drops of water at the gifts so carefully arranged on the ledge. "I think I'd like to leave them here," she finally said. "Well, everything except the little dog. He's so comical! And later, when we're old and think that maybe these things didn't really happen to us, we can look at the little dog and remember that it was all real."

"Then that's what we'll do," Remi said.

"I've got to tell you something," Aderonke said.

"What's that?"

"I'm sorry I teased you so. I know I was terrible, and I didn't mean to hurt you. I'm also sorry I kept accepting gifts from all those suitors. I wasn't that interested in any of them, although some of them were nice enough. I certainly didn't need any of their gifts. You'll laugh at me, but do you know that the only gift I received that I cared anything about was that writing paper and pen you gave me? And the thing is, I already had writing paper and a very fancy gold pen my father had bought me in the city. It came all the way from Switzerland. But your gift was important to me because it came from you. And I also cared for it because you had thought about what kind of person I am really like underneath all my silliness. You gave me a gift—I don't exactly know how to say it—that was meant for the best in me, the best I could be. Nobody else thought of me like that. Nobody else saw who I really was. Nobody else really *looked* at me. Do you know what I mean?"

Remi nodded.

"Anyway, I'm sorry. Truly I am, and I hope you can forgive me. I blame myself because of all that has happened to you...."

"Aderonke," Remi said, "you mustn't blame yourself! You silly girl, don't you know yet that this was the best thing that could have happened to me? If I had not been beaten up by those thugs and thrown into the ocean, I would not have ended up on this island. And if I had not ended up on this island, I would not have learned to do the things I can do now. You know what some of those things are."

"Oh, yes, Remi, I certainly do! It's not that you learned to make a home for yourself where there were no tools to work with, no elders to advise you, and no help of any kind. I know that isn't the most important thing you learned. I couldn't have come to find you if you hadn't learned the other things." Aderonke cast her eyes down, suddenly shy. "I mean, it looks to me as if you've somehow learned… but I don't know how anyone can learn such things without a master. But you have, haven't you, Remi? You've learned to be a medicine man, I think."

Remi took hold of Aderonke's chin and made her look at him. "Well, a little bit, Aderonke. And I can feel that there will be more. It isn't just the dreams, you know. I can look down into the earth and up into the sky and see things. And I hear things.… Well, I suppose I can't really explain it very well. And I probably shouldn't. Do you think your grandfather would talk to me? I'd like to know what I should do next, what I should expect."

"I think so. You know that dear man who gave me Paradise—you haven't seen her yet, but she's beautiful!—and who arranged this trip to find you? He thinks Grandfather was responsible for everything. The more I think about it, the more I think he's right. We certainly couldn't have done it without Grandfather's help. I really believe he'll talk to you. Oh, Remi! Do you know that I'm so proud of you?"

Remi responded with a new verse of Aderonke's song:

> Aderonke, Aderonke, Aderonke!
> How strong and beautiful you have grown!
> How brave and faithful you have been!
> Now there is nothing to keep us apart!
> Now there is nothing that can hurt us!
> We will be together every day of our lives!
> We will be together forever, Aderonke!

And Aderonke smiled. She pointed at Remi's chest and answered with a song of her own:

> You are my Remi, my promised husband!
> You are my Remi, my promised husband!
> How strong and handsome you have grown!
> How brave and faithful you have been!
> Now there is nothing to keep us apart!
> Now there is nothing that can hurt us!

We will be together every day of our lives!
We will be together forever, my Remi!

You are a man, no longer a boy!
You are a man, a complete man at that!
You are far better than what you have been!
No one knows how much better you will be!
You will be the envy of our village;
You will be the envy of the world around you.
You have laid a foundation for yourself.
You have laid a foundation for our family.
You have laid a foundation of strength.
You have laid a foundation of knowledge.

You are my Remi, my promised husband!
You are my Remi, my promised husband!
You have earned the greatest respect.
You have learned without a teacher.
You have skills that came from no master.
You have reached across the ocean.
You can make the impossible happen.
You can do what others cannot do.
You can do more than all the suitors.
You can do more than those who know so much.

Every problem brings with it a blessing.
Every problem brings out the best in you.
You have brought about solutions to your
    problems.

You have found solutions to our problems.
Do you believe you will be great?
I believe you will be very great!
Your name will be famous, you wait and see!
Your name will spread far and wide, wait and
　　see!
You are worth more than one can imagine!
You are worth more than a world full of suitors!

You are my Remi, my promised husband!
You are my Remi, my promised husband!
All who are poor will hear of your achievement;
You will give courage to all who hear of you.
All who know little will hear of your knowledge;
You will stir the intellect of all who hear of
　　you.

Everyone said you were a poor farmer;
Everyone said you were nothing but a peasant.
You thought you were nothing but a poor man;
You thought you were nothing but a peasant.
Now you have overcome impossible odds;
Now you have achieved the unachievable.

Everyone said you were a dreamer;
Everyone said you wanted the impossible.
You thought you were nothing but a dreamer;
You thought you wanted the impossible.

Through your dreaming, you have done the im-
        possible;
Through your dreaming, you have brought me to
        you.

Your dreaming is your talent, my husband!
Your dreaming is a gift of God, my husband!
Your dreaming will bring you prosperity!
Your dreaming will bring you great fame!
Your dreaming has brought you your wife!
Your dreaming will bring you the future!

You are Remi, my promised husband!
You are Remi, my promised husband!
How strong and handsome you have grown!
How brave and faithful you have been!
Now there is nothing to keep us apart!
Now there is nothing that can hurt us!
We will be together every day of our lives!
We will be together forever, my Remi!

And Waterfall flapped around the little clearing, crying "We will be together forever, Aderonke!"

If Remi had not already been transformed by the events that had happened to him, this song of Aderonke's would have transformed him. As it was, he could feel only a great and profound joy like the kind felt when he was most in tune with his newly discovered gifts.

When Remi was finally able to speak, he blinked his eyes hard and looked around the clearing. "I wonder what it will be like to be home," he said.

"I wonder, too," Aderonke answered. "I haven't been there since I 'died,' you know! And we still don't know who it was that tried to kill you."

"But I do!" Remi answered. "Those four thugs were pretty free with their talk; I guess they figured it didn't matter because I was dead. It was the palm-wine seller and the pharmacist. The thugs were from a village about a hundred and twenty miles away. I don't remember the name of it right now, but one of them mentioned it, and if I hear it again, I'll recognize it. I rather imagine that your friend the police officer is going to get a chance to cover himself with glory when I give him the information."

"Oh, Remi, that's a good thing! You know, I wondered for a while if he had done it himself, but he was so concerned about me when I was busy 'dying' that I hated to trick him. He was the one who managed somehow to come up with that helicopter. It was a wonderful way to get me out of there with everyone thinking I was deathly ill, but he really believed I was. He didn't do it to rescue me from all the suitors; he did it because he believed I was really sick. He's a little full of himself, but he's actually a nice young man at heart. I hope he finds a good wife. I'm glad you'll be able to tell him what he needs to know to catch the criminals. Six of them! That will make a name for him in the district. It must be pretty hard being a police officer where almost nothing ever happens and where you never get a chance to be noticed!"

"You don't think he'll be out to get me now that you are to be my wife?" Remi asked.

"No, I don't think so. He'll be so happy to be noticed. Everyone in town will think him enormously clever, and I think he's likely to get some good offers of marriage if he hasn't gotten any already. His father is an important man, and this high-profile case will make his reputation. If anything, I think he'll be glad to make friends with you!"

"I'm relieved to hear that....You know, Aderonke, I haven't any money or property. I'm afraid we're going to be poor, and you're not used to that."

"Don't you say that, Remi!" Aderonke exclaimed. "In the first place, my father has a lot of property. I'm his only child, and he will give quite a bit of it to me for a wedding gift. His brothers are both dead, so now he has only Nimi. When he dies—God forbid!— he will leave most of it to you so that you can take care of my mother. You will be a rich man, Remi!"

"I don't want to be rich just because your father had only one child."

"Well, you won't be! You'll be rich because you are intelligent and handsome and persistent and brave and faithful and a whole lot of other wonderful things. You'll also be rich because I choose you out of all the men in the world for my husband, and I can give you what I please, but you would get nothing if you weren't all those things. And don't forget Grandfather."

"What do you mean?"

"I mean that Grandfather will show you how to use your great gifts. My grandfather is a wealthy man, and he got that way by using his gifts. Would you believe he actually has money invested in the capital and other places?"

"No! I didn't think he'd ever been more than a few miles from his home village."

"He hasn't, but my father invests money for him, and he gets a good return on it. Grandfather can't read and write, but he's very glad my father can!"

"Maybe he won't be willing to teach me his craft...."

"Remi, if I hear you say one more negative thing like that, I'm going to scream! You used to talk like that. You used to think of yourself like that. But no more! I can see that you don't really think of yourself like that anymore, so I won't let you talk that way. I won't!" And Aderonke pounded her fist on the rock so hard that she yelped.

"All right! Never again!" Remi said with a laugh. "Still...I suppose I just feel strange about going back to the village. Everyone thinks I'm dead. While I was here, all I could think of was getting back to you, but I hadn't thought much about what would happen afterward."

"I think we can just trust God for that," Aderonke said firmly.

Remi took her hand and agreed, "That's a good idea. I prayed and prayed right here every day, and now I have you back with me. When we've come so far, how can we doubt that everything will work out okay? Let's say a farewell prayer, shall we?"

"I think that's the best thing to do," Aderonke answered. "Will you do it?"

"Sure," Remi said, and he began to pray aloud, "O God, the Creator of all things—even our challenges are known to you. And because you create us as well as our challenges, we know that you will make us the people you want us to be. We are convinced that you would not lead us so far only to let us fail in the future. We commit everything to your hands. We thank you that there is a purpose in all things, and we thank you that this is the day you have appointed to bring us back home again. This is not the end for us, but the beginning, and we are making this beginning in your strength. Amen."

Remi turned to Aderonke and said, "We will be married after we return to the village, but I want to pledge myself to you here in this place because it is sacred to you."

Remi then sang this new chant for Aderonke:

Aderonke, I love you more than anything.
You come first in my life, Aderonke.
I'd go through fire if you wanted me to.
I'd go through torrents if you wanted me to.
I'd sail alone if you wanted me to.
I'd walk or trot or run if you wanted me to.
I can be sleepless all night if you wish me to.
I can do anything at all if you wish me to.

You are my companion; you'll always be so.
You are my companion in all my happiness.
You are my companion in all my sorrow.
You are my companion even in my dreams!

I'll remain faithful when the going is tough.
I'll remain faithful when trials befall us.
I'll remain faithful when things are too easy.
I'll remain faithful when life brings us joy.

I will remain faithful to you.
I will remain faithful, my love.
I will remain faithful to my Aderonke.
I will remain faithful forever.

# FOURTEEN

After resing for a few days at Nimi's house, Remi and Aderonke started the three-day trip home. Aderonke's parents had gone on ahead, bearing with them some information for the police officer, but no one else was told that Remi and Aderonke were alive. Thus, when they arrived in town, they created quite a stir.

One elderly lady was convinced they were ghosts and went shrieking down the street to warn her neighbors. The children were interested mostly because Aderonke and Remi were dressed in very fine, brand-new clothing, and both of them carried leather suitcases, just like real world travelers. Even if they thought the couple might be a pair of ghosts, the children didn't seem particularly worried; they could smell a good story in a village where nothing much ever happened.

By the time Remi and Aderonke had walked to Aderonke's parents' home, there was quite a crowd following them. As they passed through the market, they collected all kinds of people, including some of those who had come to sell their wares.

Some were curious because both Remi and Aderonke were supposed to have died. Some were curious because of a wonderful coincidence: Only two days earlier, the police officer had arrested the pharmacist and the palm-wine seller for attempted murder, and just this morning, a truck had brought four thugs to be locked up in the town's tiny jail. Some were curious because they knew of Remi's courtship of Aderonke, and they wondered if she had chosen him out of all her suitors. Some were curious simply because of the travelers' fancy clothing and their big leather suitcases.

Still others were curious because Aderonke's parents had arrived in town only a few days before, looking as if their faces would break and hardly speaking to anyone. They correctly guessed that there must be an interesting tale here somewhere!

In any event, by the time they reached Aderonke's house, the crowd was so large and noisy that neither Remi nor Aderonke could hear the people who greeted them, and it was nearly impossible to walk.

Of course, no one commented on the fact that both of them were supposed to be dead—as if they might disappear like real ghosts if anyone said anything!

Aderonke's dog came out and barked ferociously at everyone, but he leaped happily around Remi and nearly knocked Aderonke over in his joy at seeing her again. Both Remi and Aderonke were greatly relieved to squeeze inside the house and shut the door.

Remi was astonished to find his parents and sister in the sitting room with Aderonke's parents. They had all missed one another tremendously over the two years Remi had been marooned on the island. There were joyful greetings all around.

"You see, Remi?" Aderonke's father's said. "I told you everything would work out right!"

The families had little time to themselves before the commotion outside became too great to ignore. People were dancing and singing, but even louder than that was the incessant chattering. By this time, rumors were running wild.

Remi had not been dead, of course. Instead he was working covertly with the police officer to trap the pharmacist and the palm-wine seller and their henchmen in a smuggling ring! Or Remi and Aderonke had been dead, but Aderonke's grandfather brought them both back to life again! Or Remi had been dead, but Aderonke had not. Aderonke's grandfather raised Remi from the dead, but Aderonke spent the last two years nursing him back to health. Or Aderonke had been dead, but

Remi had not. He escaped from his captors, who were afraid they would lose their pay if they admitted it, and in making his way back to his village, Remi passed through Aderonke's grandfather's village. There he discovered that Aderonke was dead, and he studied magical healing incantations with her grandfather. Together the two of them raised Aderonke from the dead!

"Hello! Hello! What's going on here?" the police officer bellowed over the noise of the crowd. People stepped back to let him pass. He had gone up in everyone's estimation over the past few days. It was now widely known that he had caught six criminals. Some wondered if maybe there were more of them, and there were only six in the village jail because the jail could hardly hold that many at one time. Maybe there were hundreds more in jails all over the country thanks to this village's police officer.

At any rate, the crowd quieted down somewhat. "What's going on? Why is everybody hanging around this house and disturbing the peace?"

The police officer did not sound fierce at all. He knew very well what was going on, and he was so eager to see Aderonke and make certain that she was all right that he could hardly keep his excitement hidden.

"It's Aderonke and Remi!" someone answered. "They are alive and have returned to our village!

And from the looks of his clothes, Remi is rich!" This generated a new buzz in the crowd.

"Oh, they are, are they? Well, let me just see about that. I have some official business with Paul and Eli." The police officer stepped up to the door, and Aderonke's father let him in.

After greeting the older people, the police officer turned to Aderonke. "I see you are well, Aderonke," he said, breaking into a huge smile. "I could not be happier."

"Thank you," Aderonke said. "I could hardly be happier myself! Did my parents tell you what happened?"

"Yes, they did. You gave me quite a fright, you know! How wicked of you to pretend to be sick and then to pretend to die, and me here pining away for you!" But the police officer did not look at all disapproving as he said these words.

"Let him tell you how he has pined away!" Eli said with a laugh. "He has not only a pretty wife but also a little son!"

"Now I know I'm not the worst tease in this village!" Aderonke said. "I'm so glad to hear you have started a family. I'll visit your wife and baby as soon as I get settled in. But I hear you have made a name for yourself in the last few days."

"Indeed I have, and it's all thanks to Remi."

"That's all right," Remi hastily said. "Don't tell anyone where you got the information. A police officer's lot is hard enough without having someone else steal what little glory there is! I'd prefer that everyone recognize the hard work you've put into this case."

"Thank you, Remi," the police officer answered. "It certainly is true that we police officers have a hard lot. Do you hear that crowd outside?"

"How could we miss it?" everyone asked in unison.

"What do you think about making a little speech?" the police officer asked. "You know, just telling people a little of what happened and letting them know you're not ghosts!"

Remi looked at Aderonke and asked her, "What do you think?"

"We're going to have to say something sooner or later," she said. "We may as well tell everyone at once instead of having to tell our story a hundred times over!"

"Do you have something we could use for a little platform?" the police officer asked.

Aderonke's father fetched a flat wooden box. The police officer moved the crowd back somewhat, promising them that they would soon be treated to the most astonishing news ever heard in the village.

"Quiet there! Quiet!" the police officer shouted importantly, as Aderonke and Remi came out of he house and climbed up on the platform.

Aderonke's father stepped up: "Dear friends and neighbors, I want to tell you how happy I am this day to welcome my beloved daughter, Aderonke, back home. She and her promised husband, Remi—"

At this, the crowd erupted into more noise. Aderonke's father raised his hand and waited for the noise to subside.

He continued, "She and her promised husband, Remi, have been through a great adventure, and I will let them tell the story. And I would like to suggest that after we have heard their story, we should have a feast. I have been preparing a little something for this great occasion, and I am sure you will enjoy it. Thank you."

There was great applause following this announcement, and the crowd settled down to listen to Remi's story.

"My future father-in-law does me great honor," he began, "and I thank him for it. But he has done me much greater honor for the past two years. Let me explain this to you. I am sure no one else knew that my parents and Aderonke's parents had agreed that we might marry. At the time, I was a very poor man with no prospects, and as you all know, Aderonke had many suitors. She was a lovely girl, but she was still very much a child and not yet ready to settle down in marriage. But when we met, a very strong spirit developed between us. Aderonke was about to return to her suitors those gifts they had given her, and she was finally ready to announce her betrothal to me.

"But then two of the suitors, men of low cunning and no morals, saw what was happening and decided to get rid of me. They hired four thugs from a nearby village to knock me over the head and throw me in the sea. And the thugs performed their commission—except that I was not at all dead and did not intend to die. I nearly died in the ocean, however, being adrift for three days and holding on to a bit of floating debris. I would never have thought a man could live so long at sea without even a boat, but I believe it was Aderonke's spirit that kept me alive.

"I washed up on a coral reef that surrounded a little island many many miles to the northwest. There I remained for two years. In that entire time, I never saw a single ship. The island was deserted; it didn't even have any mammals on it—only birds and reptiles. Every kind of fish you could imagine lived in the coral reef. I was alone and without tools, not even a knife. Everything I needed I fashioned from the shells and stones and wood and vines around me. I had to find out what was good to eat because the only familiar things growing there were not enough to keep me alive. I had to devise shelter and make the tools with which to do the job. And do you know what kept me alive?" Remi paused dramatically.

"It was Aderonke," he said. "I wanted nothing so much as to return to her. She was my life. Every day I prayed that we would be reunited. I tried to devise ways to leave the island, but I had nothing from which to make a sail, and I knew from experience that the current that had brought me there was quite strong. And I had no expertise in the ways of the sea. So every night I lit a signal fire, and every day I damped it down to make a lot of smoke, and all day and all night I hoped for a miracle to happen. And then the miracle happened. I will let Aderonke tell you about it."

Aderonke stepped up on the box. She smiled at Remi and then began to speak.

"I suppose you wonder what happened to me. Well, when Remi was kidnapped, I thought he was dead. And I also thought—I had reason to believe, you see, because our police officer here is so very good at working such things out—that it was one or more of my suitors who had done this terrible thing. But I didn't know which one, and naturally my parents were alarmed. We asked my grandfather for advice, and he told us what to do. I pretended to be very sick—and this was very easy for me, because I was so unhappy thinking Remi had died. I was taken to the district hospital, and from there I snuck away to live with Aunt Nimi in the capital. But my parents spread the word that I had died, believing that this would help the police officer in his investigations. And it did. He was able to piece together the evidence, and as you know, he arrested the culprits just a few days ago. We all owe him a great debt of thanks."

At this point, Aderonke turned toward the police officer and started clapping, and the crowd burst out with applause. The police officer bowed and smiled and looked exceedingly important and pleased with himself.

"Of course, I was very sad living with Aunt Nimi. I was going to the university, though I am not really all that fond of books, because I had determined that I would never marry anyone but Remi. And if he was dead, I would not marry at all. So I would have to support myself, and I had decided I would be a teacher because there is always a great need for teachers. I was working hard at my studies when something interesting began to happen. I won't bore you with all the details, but I began to have strange dreams. These dreams were about Remi, and they were not like the dreams one might have of the dead. I consulted my aunt, and she wrote to my parents, who consulted my grandfather again.... Now, you already know that my grandfather is a highly skilled medicine man."

The crowd murmured assent.

"And this very kind and very great man advised me on what to do. I was able to follow his advice, and because of it, I was able to discover where Remi was. With the help of my uncle, we managed to get transportation, and the long and the short of it is that we located Remi very quickly. Now I can tell you that Remi used to be a peasant, but he will no longer be a peasant. You will soon see for yourselves the things that Remi has learned and become during our absence. Now let's all get ready to have a celebration!"

Aderonke bowed and smiled, and the crowd once again burst into applause and cheers.

Aderonke had purposely not said anything at all about what Remi had learned and become while on the island. They had agreed not to mention this to anyone until Remi had spoken with Aderonke's grandfather. Let the neighbors wonder if Remi had discovered buried treasure!

The homecoming celebration was everything a celebration should be. Aderonke's father had been well prepared. Palm wine flowed freely, there was much dancing, and people were already beginning to make up songs about Remi and Aderonke's adventures. Because the couple had left out most of the details, their neighbors were free to add anything colorful that might make the story better, and everyone liked that because it was fun to embellish the tale and to outdo one another in making it even more fantastic.

Most of all, there was food. Aderonke wondered whether her father had completely emptied the markets for miles around. She had never seen so much food. When she commented on it, her father said, "Wait until your wedding! Just wait! This is nothing, let me tell you! When you get married, *then* we will have a feast!"

Of course, all the neighbors crowded around Aderonke and Remi, asking questions and trying to find out more. But they answered with cheery generalizations, praising each other to the skies and pointing out what a wonderful job the police officer had done in catching the malefactors. Remi regaled people with long descriptions of every kind of fish in the coral reef, and Aderonke talked about her future with Remi. But they politely deflected any questions about the dreams or about what her grandfather had advised, changing the subject to something else equally interesting.

Remi and Aderonke reiterated to their friends and neighbors that they were not sorry they had gone through such a difficult time. The criminals had been caught, their love had been confirmed, they had both grown a great deal through their suffering, and they had been granted a most wonderful miracle. Now they were glad to be home, and they felt extremely hopeful about the future. They knew for certain that there would always be a way through any difficulty; they were convinced that there would always be hope—not so much that where there's life, there's hope, but where there's hope, there's life.

Remi called himself the luckiest man in the village to have Aderonke for his wife—not because she was beautiful, but because she was so good and faithful and committed to him. Otherwise, he would never have gotten off the island. Eventually she would grow old, and she would no longer be considered so beautiful by most, but what was inside her could only grow stronger and more beautiful every day.

For her part, Aderonke avowed that she was the luckiest girl in the village to have Remi for her husband—not because he was strong and handsome, but because of the strength of his love and of his character. Otherwise, she would never have found him again. Eventually he would grow old, and he would no longer be considered so strong and handsome, but his love and his fine character could only grow stronger every day.

Both Remi and Aderonke encouraged all the younger guests who were planning on marriage to look inside the person they wished to marry. They advised: Determine always to be faithful in love, and never give up no matter what difficulties life unexpectedly presents. After all, who would have believed that a poor peasant like Remi would come to marry the most beautiful and richest young lady in town? Who would have believed childish, silly

Aderonke would rescue her promised husband from his terrible isolation?

The party went well into the night, with everyone having a good time. It was past midnight when Remi and his family took leave of Aderonke and her family. Tomorrow they would go to consult Aderonke's grandfather.

# FIFTEEN

The very next morning, Eli, Aderonke, and Remi went to the nearby village where Aderonke's grandfather lived. Eli greeted her father with great reverence and spoke to him privately for a time. Then he asked to see the young people.

"Ah, Aderonke! I am so glad to see you!" the old man said, lifting Aderonke to her feet and folding her in his arms. "You have grown up into a fine young woman. Tell me about yourself, my dear."

"Oh, thank you, Grandfather," Aderonke answered. "Yes, I think I have grown up at last! You know everything that has happened to me. In fact, I suspect that you know more about it than I do myself. What can I tell you that you don't already know?"

Aderonke's grandfather smiled and said, "You are perceptive as well as beautiful, Aderonke! Well, I suppose there's not much you can tell me...except perhaps about your bird. Did you have much trouble finding the right one?"

"A little at first, Grandfather. The market didn't have anything at all, but a friend of Aunt Nimi's husband turned out to have the most beautiful aviary. I bet he has the best collection of birds anywhere in Africa if not in the whole world! And he just *gave* me the bird. She's a beautiful red macaw. She was a baby when I got her, but she's all feathered out now and absolutely, astonishingly beautiful."

"I hope you brought her home with you."

"Actually, Paradise—that's her name—and Waterfall—that's Remi's parrot—came home with my parents. We knew there would be chaos when we returned to the village. We wanted them to get a chance to settle in peacefully first—but that may have been a mistake. Remi's mother said that Waterfall wouldn't eat or chatter or anything. He just sat in his cage until Remi came home. And Paradise was even worse! She tried to eat her way out of her cage, and they had a terrible time with her!"

"You must be very careful with these birds from now on," her grandfather warned. "Yes, it was a mistake to send them home ahead of you. They will be very dependent on your company, both because they are pets and because of the special function they have served. And you must know that they may serve similar functions in the future."

"Oh!" Aderonke drew in her breath, her hand going to her mouth. "Do you—I mean—are you going to…?"

"You know perfectly well what I mean," her grandfather said. "You have shown a great deal of intelligence and determination in the last several months. Don't start acting like an empty-headed girl again!" His words were harsh, but his facial expression was gentle.

"Yes, Grandfather," Aderonke said meekly.

"Now I want to talk to your young man."

Remi spent four hours talking with Aderonke's grandfather. After the first ten minutes had passed, Aderonke was certain that their conversation must be going well because her grandfather was not a person to mince words. If he talked this long with someone, it was because he had something meaningful to say and because he thought the person was worth his time.

Aderonke's grandfather invited them to stay for a late lunch, and it was nearly sunset when they returned to her home.

"Now, Remi," Aderonke said when they had made themselves comfortable in the sitting room, "please tell me all about what Grandfather said to you. I am dying of curiosity!"

"Then you will just have to die, poor Aderonke!" Remi said with a laugh. "I'm afraid it was all man talk!"

"You're not going to tell me *anything*! How can you be so mean, Remi?"

"Well, I suppose I'd better tell you what my plans are. After all, they involve you." Remi was infuriatingly calm and nonchalant.

"Yes?" Aderonke felt as if she would burst. "Yes, what *is* it?"

"Of course, we are going to get married. You know that. And, of course, your parents will want to do everything the old-fashioned way, the traditional way. Those ways are dying out now, and more and more people don't seem to keep the old customs. But your grandfather and your parents will want to do things the old way, don't you think?"

"Oh, certainly! And that's what I want to do! Why, we could have gotten married in the city if we weren't going to do it right! Yes, by all means."

"And, of course, it will take a little time to get ready for that. I don't know precisely, but I suppose you will have things to consult the older women about....Your father and mine will get together, and your mother and mine will have a lot to do, don't you think?"

"Yes, of course. It's funny. I hadn't really thought much about it what we would do after we actually got home! But that's exactly what we should do."

"All right. Meanwhile, I will be spending quite a bit of time with your grandfather—"

"Oh, Remi!" Aderonke interrupted excitedly.

"—and then after we are married," Remi continued, "we will go to live with him for a time because I have a lot to learn."

"Oh, how wonderful!" Tears streamed down Aderonke's face.

"I will tell you this, Aderonke," Remi said seriously. "Your grandfather told me that medicine men are born, not made. He said people are born with the talent and that it comes out either because they are trained when they are young or because some terrible event takes place that forces the talent to show. He has known both kinds. Not every young person who is taken into training succeeds; in fact, he said only a small percentage of them do. And for those to whom something terrible has happened that forced them to use their talent, it is often extremely hard to bring it under control and use it consistently for good. He believes I was forced to gain much of this control there on the island because otherwise my newly discovered talent would have driven me mad. He is certain I will do well, following in his footsteps. You know, Aderonke, I am marrying into a family with good connections. I could get any kind of education or training I want and enter any profession I have in mind, but I am pursuing this profession because it chose me even before I was born. This is what I am. I would rather be a great man in this little village doing what our ancestors have always done than be a mediocre government official wearing gold braid on my uniform."

"Oh, Remi!" Aderonke sniffled. "You can't imagine how proud I am! I know you will be a great man. I think you're a great man already!"

The next day, Aderonke's parents called her over to them for a serious conversation.

"Aderonke," her father began, "you are our only daughter. You've been out in the big world for some time now and seen the way many other people live. You have been through such trials and shown yourself intelligent and capable. We love you dearly, as you are our only treasure. Both you and Remi are entirely precious to us, and we are glad you are marrying someone of such fine character and ability. We could not ask for any better for you. But we must ask you to allow us to conduct your wedding in the old, traditional way. This would mean so very much to us. All your life, we have looked forward to the day of your marriage, and this is the best opportunity of our lives to host the greatest festival this village has ever seen. We want everyone to come: our friends and relatives, people we know in the city, and people from around here. We want your wedding to be the wedding of the century! Will you do that for us?"

"Why, of course!" Aderonke exclaimed. "How could you ever doubt it? As you know, Grandfather will train Remi to become a medicine man. How traditional a profession can a person have? Of course we will have a traditional wedding! Yes, make it the greatest celebration this village has ever experienced. After all, it's going to be the greatest celebration of my whole life, too!"

"Wonderful!" her father said. "We had been concerned about it. You have spent more time in the city during your life than you have here in the village, and we hoped you weren't completely given over to everything modern! Now I know you are eager to move forward; you and Remi have waited a long and difficult time. We will make the arrangements as fast as we can. Whatever you would like to suggest, we will do it that way. You and Remi decide on the date you would like, and we will find a way to get everything done before then, okay?"

"Fine, fine! We will make the date far enough away that you can get everything done easily. Plus, Remi will have to be in training for a while, so perhaps we should consult Grandfather as to the best time. After we have waited so long, a little longer won't matter. And all of us will have so much to do that I'm sure the time will go quickly. For one thing, I need to create a good lyric to sing. I'll need to talk to several of the women and get some ideas, and I'll have to learn the traditional parts. I have some ideas, too, for some original parts.The cusotm is dying out and I want to do it right."

"You're certainly right there," Eli said. "Traditional weddings are becoming a thing of the past. It's a terrible blow to our culture in every respect, and the marriage lyric is no exception. But everyone looks up to the rare brides who still sing the marriage lyric. You've been away so long! Honoring the traditions will make your marriage even stronger. I'm afraid some of the customs have been totally forgotten, but we will talk to some of the oldest ladies and see what we can find out. Did you know your father and I were married in the city?"

"No!" Aderonke was shocked.

"Indeed, we were," her father said. "Your grandfather was very angry for a good long time! But your mother was always his favorite child, so he eventually forgave her. When she was young, she had a hankering for European customs. She's learned a little better now, I think!"

Eli laughed and admitted, "I certainly have! I've learned you can take a lot of good things from any culture as long as they fit your own life. But when it comes to the big transitions in your life—marriage and the birth of children, for instance—it's better to hold to the old ways. You can imagine how pleased I am that you want a truly traditional wedding, and I'll do everything I can possibly do to make it the best ever!"

"Now, Aderonke," her father said, putting on his most serious look, "we want to talk to you about something else. You are our only child. Remi is a talented man who will someday make a great name for himself, but he presently has no property at all. Now you know, too, that your mother and I are well off. I own very good property here, in many other villages, on farms, and in the city. Your mother and I are going to keep this little house and garden here in the village. For your marriage settlement, we are giving to you and Remi all our other property. Remi will not have to chop wood to support you, and he will be able to take all the time he needs in preparing for his profession." At this point, Aderonke's father wiped his brow and cleared his throat.

"You are so generous!" Aderonke said. "You've always been the kindest, most loving parents, even when I was a silly adolescent who didn't let you have a moment's peace! How can I ever thank you?"

"Um...well...um!" her father stammered.

"What your father means, dear," Eli said, "is that for you and Remi and your children to be happy is the greatest thanks we can possibly have. You are making a fine marriage, and it will give us great joy to see you happy." Eli gave her child the long hug that mothers give daughters who will soon be married.

"You are the greatest parents in the whole world," Aderonke said. "You've always been generous and you're giving a tremendous gift. And I have learned to rely more on myself now. I would prefer that people didn't think everything I have came from my parents and that I didn't work for any of it. But I've learned something else, too. I've learned that everyone has something to give. Remi had so little money that all he could give me in the way of things was some writing paper and a pen, and I already had writing paper and a pen. But I treasured his gift because he looked inside me and saw what was there, and gave me a gift that was just perfect for that. I will treasure your gift for the same reason. You give it not just to shower something on me; you give it because you know Remi is my chosen husband and that this gift will enable him to take up the most honorable of professions. You know I want that for him, and that is why you are giving it to me. Had I married any other man, you would not have given me such a lavish gift. All I can say is thank you so much. From the bottom of my heart, thank you."

"You have learned from your experience," Eli said. "I've heard it said that experience is the best teacher. Sometimes it is the only teacher! I know you will be the best possible wife for Remi. An industrious child is the pride of her parents, and I know that your acceptance of this gift will not make you lazy. You are no longer a spoiled girl. You set out to make a living for yourself in the city, and when the chance came to rescue Remi from his island, you overcame every obstacle. There is no doubt in our minds that you will use every effort to build a good life for your husband and children and that you will use this property not just for your own family but for others, too. You have always had a generous spirit, Aderonke."

"And a foolish one," Aderonke answered, shaking her head. "It has taken me a long time to grow up. And I'm afraid Remi suffered badly for it. And so did you."

"Not a bit," her father said. "We have learned some things from this experience, too. Before, we wanted you to have a good marriage, and pretty much all we thought mattered was that the young man have good prospects because we did not want someone

marrying you for your money. We didn't think much
beyond that. Then Remi came along and was so
obviously sincere that we began to change our
minds about what was important. We should really
be ashamed of ourselves, you know, because your
mother and I were not chosen for each other by
our families. Now I think it is a very good thing for
families to agree on the marriage of their children,
and I wish we had been a little more thoughtful of
our parents when we were younger. But there we
were, thinking not so much of you as of what other
people might call a 'good match.' Well, Daughter,
we all keep learning all our lives!"

Later that afternoon, Remi came to visit Paul. As
Remi left, Paul handed him a large sum of money
for Remi's parents—to help them prepare for the
wedding and make some improvements on their
meager property.

"And don't tell them where it came from," Paul
warned. "Just tell them it's your money and that you
have come by it honestly. And tell them there will
be more available as you improve in your chosen
profession. You don't need to explain your finances
to anyone. Aderonke's property is now yours, and
you are not accountable to anyone for it."

Two years ago, Remi would have protested, claiming that he wanted to make his own way. Now he knew it was as important to accept a gift as to give one, and he thanked his future father-in-law warmly.

While the marriage preparations were under way, Remi settled in to learn from Aderonke's grandfather. Remi never spoke of what transpired between them—at least not to anyone but his own apprentices, when he himself was much older and more advanced in his profession.

Aderonke and her mother managed to find several women who could teach her the marriage lyric. For the next three weeks, Aderonke constantly listened to these women, practiced what they taught her, and then practiced some more. When she had learned all she could from them, she began to work on her own additions. If this was to be the finest wedding the village had ever seen, her marriage lyric would be the finest ever sung!

Eli, Bimpe, and Tohun immersed themselves in a flurry of activity. They attended every market day in nearby villages as well as their own, and twice Eli wrote to Aunt Nimi in the capital to see if she could find a special something. They made arrangements with the new palm-wine seller who had taken the place of the one in prison—to procure such a quantity of palm wine that he would need to subcontract a lot of the work. They procured so many kola nuts that one wondered if there were any left in the entire country...secured drummers and other entertainers from out of town in addition to the local talent... found local girls to spend the traditional four days in seclusion with Aderonke...negotiated with a man who had large plantations of yams...arranged for the delivery of six fat cows three days before the marriage...

Eli and Tohun sent messages to formally announce the date of the wedding to their closest friends. These friends would be at the watch night the night before the marriage. Eli and Tohun informed the women in their compounds and all their well-wishers. Eli wrote to her friends in the city and elsewhere throughout the district, inviting them to come for the big event. The two fathers informed their own friends, and Paul wrote a great many letters to business associates.

As their friends were informed, they sent kola nuts in acknowledgment. This was a handy custom, as it greatly increased the number of nuts available for the celebration.

In addition, Tohun8 busied herself with weaving sleeping clothes for Remi and Aderonke to use on their wedding night. And Eli, who had never much bothered with such detailed work because she always had enough money to buy whatever she wanted, spent a great deal of time and effort making some special clothes for Aderonke.

Remi's parents paid the bride price. Remi's father hired people to prepare Aderonke's parents' large farm outside of town. Toye sent men to thatch the roofs of Aderonke's parents' house and also of Aderonke's grandfather's house in the neighboring village. He sent three loads of yams to the festival of their family god, which was three weeks before the wedding, and he provided palm wine on this occasion, too. Of course, he sent the expected amount of money. These were very great expenses for a peasant family, but they were borne with little trouble because...well, because Remi had made a name for himself and had come into some money.

Remi's parents also had to supply some of the tremendous amount of food for the celebration. Ordinarily, a family and its close relatives would be able to put together all the food, but in this case, friends and neighbors had to help. Before long, practically everyone in town was busy preparing some aspect of the wedding, and the excitement grew markedly.

Aderonke had been so busy with her own preparations that she was entirely unaware of her mother making the special wedding clothes for her. When Eli called her in to look at the finished product, Aderonke was astonished. "Mother! I never dreamed that you would go to all the trouble of weaving this for me! This is the most wonderful garment of all. Thank you so much! It's beautiful! "Now you must teach me how to do this so that I will be able to weave something for my own daughter. Like you, I'll have enough money to buy anything I want—but I think Remi and I are supposed to preserve the old arts. If you can do it, I can do it! And learning from you how to weave and sew would make me feel so incredibly special!"

Aderonke hugged the wedding clothes close to her chest and smiled radiantly. Eli thought her own heart would break for happiness.

"I'm sorry I haven't taught you before now. I hadn't done any weaving myself in fifteen years, and it wasn't so easy to take it up again. But then while I was doing it, I had this extraordinary feeling of closeness, a sort of kinship with my own mother and all the other women who have done the same thing for their daughters since the beginning of time. Yes, I'll show you how."

As the wedding approached, Aderonke had to begin the dyeing of her arms and feet. Two of her friends picked lali leaves, and her mother ground them up. They were so moist that no water was added, but a little lime juice was squeezed in. Eli broke a little broomstraw and stuck that into the lali, too, so it wouldn't lose its potency.

This mixture was spread on Aderonke's hands, forearms, and feet. On the first day, her skin turned yellowish-red. She let this dry and applied some more dye three days later. Now her skin turned dark red. After another three days, she applied more dye, which turned her skin black. Aderonke rather liked the effect and continued to apply a little more dye every few days so that the coloring would remain for several weeks after her wedding.

Guests began to arrive from outlying villages and from the larger cities as well. As more guests arrived, the market vendors found themselves running out of goods. They had to bring products from their relatives and friends and even buy from other markets. All these guests had to be fed, and all of them had to give gifts to their hosts; many also bought items for themselves. The pubs and palm-wine sellers experienced a roaring business, and there was no question that everyone in town was warming up to the coming celebration. Thus, Aderonke's wedding became famous throughout the district before it even took place.

Aderonke had been worried about the reactions of her former suitors—but all of them (even the murderous pharmacist and palm-wine seller) had married and fathered children during Aderonke's absence. Aderonke secretly sent generous gifts of money to the pharmacist's and palm-wine seller's unfortunate wives and children. Their neighbors had been none-too-kind to them after their husbands were arrested, but Aderonke spread the word among her friends that she considered them entirely innocent of what their husbands had done and that she did not want them to be ill-treated. She invited them to the wedding, and was so openly kind to them that these women and their children were no longer ostracized by their neighbors.

Seven days before the date of the marriage, all of Aderonke's close female relatives moved in with the family to help out with the increasing workload. Because the house was completely full, they set up a large tent outside for the ladies to sleep in, and there was a great deal of giggling and chattering and gossiping both there and wherever the women were working.

Nimi—the sophisticated, citified, educated Aunt Nimi—was having a terrific time going barefoot and wearing only the most traditional of clothing, immersing her arms up to the elbows in pots of this and baskets of that, and doing all the chores she had never wanted to do when she was a girl. She laughed at her own clumsiness and ignorance, but everyone noticed that Nimi quickly caught on to any task and was a very competent worker. The women's respect for education and sophistication rose accordingly.

Five days before the wedding, Aderonke's household grew again. All her unmarried friends—which meant all the girls in the village who were older than six and younger than eighteen—came to live with her. They were given a special portion of the kitchen to do their cooking in; they had their own firewood, cooking pots, and utensils; and they were given special food set aside only for them. Aderonke's father set up another tent for them to sleep in, and he filled it with everything possible to make them all comfortable.

With all these people around, there were some tense moments, and sometimes Aderonke had to kneel before a group of quarreling older women and beg them to settle their quarrel. They always stated their cases to her, but she was afraid to make any judgments in these matters because she worried that she might offend someone. On the other hand, she looked so pretty and appealing when she tried to soothe them that most of the time those involved broke up the quarrel with laughter and hugs, feeling a little ashamed of themselves.

In their tent, the girls listened to Aderonke practice her marriage lyric so that they would be able to do the same when their own wedding days came. They all admired Aderonke so much that her wedding helped reestablish the older customs for village marriages. These girls were especially impressed with her serious attention to every detail of the lyric. Aderonke also had plenty of opportunities to listen to other lyrics sung by female guests as they helped out, and she determined to memorize all of them so that they would remain part of the village's shared cultural lore.

Four days before the wedding, all the neighbors' houses were crammed with out-of-town guests. Luckily, the police officer offered his own large home and that of his father, which was the largest in town.

In addition to the six fat cows, which arrived on the third day before the wedding, there were several pigs and numerous goats to be prepared. All the men in the village worked on the butchering, and all the women worked on the cooking. The younger people did most of the actual work, while the elders demonstrated, advised, instructed, and supervised.

Two days before the wedding, massive quantities of palm wine began to arrive from vendors spread far and wide; the merchant had been quite nervous until every last drop of the order had arrived.

The drummers and entertainers had been performing every evening. In addition to the usual singers, drummers, flutists, and dancers, Aderonke's father had arranged for a troupe of acrobats, who were extremely popular with the assembled multitude.

The third day before the wedding was watch night, an all-night party and dance. When the drummers saw Remi and his entourage approaching from a distance, they left the guests and met the bridegroom. On their way, the guests pasted money on the drummers' foreheads to ensure good drumming and good luck. The women came out of Aderonke's house and joined the procession, and Remi pasted money on their foreheads. The younger women entertained the company, chanting ballads and dancing.

This party went on all night, with dancing and singing, drinking of palm wine and the eating of every delicious kind of food. Aderonke was especially delighted to find her most honored guest: a man in a very fancy naval uniform with lots of gold braid. Greeting her like a long-lost daughter, he presented her with a cage containing two tiny green lovebirds.

Of course, the parrots had to join the celebration. Paradise and Waterfall flew in circles around the guests, rode on the shoulders of Remi and Aderonke, chattered out love messages, and even kissed each other when they thought no one was looking. In their eyes, they were getting married too, and the festivities were as much about them as about their human comrades.

The following day was an all-day party at Aderonke's house in honor of her family. As the guests consumed prodigious amounts of food and palm wine, the drumming went on all day, and every inch of the house and yard was full of people. They even spilled out into the street. At this party, the drummers showed off their knowledge of the ancestry of most of those present, chanting their histories and using the talking drum to praise the guests and Aderonke's family.

The younger people began to join in with the professional dancers. One young man or woman would get up, bow to his elders, and begin to dance; then another would get up and join him or her, honoring the first dancer. Before long, a great many people were dancing. The older dancers were especially honored; people bowed or knelt to them and pasted money on their foreheads.

The drummers and other entertainers were honored not only with money but with clothing. When a family's history was recited, the head of that family might give one of the drummers a new fancy cap. Instead of laying these gifts aside, the entertainers donned these rewards on the spot.

In the late afternoon, three people carried Aderonke's special clothes, jewelry, and shoes to a house on the market square. Aderonke went too, accompanied by another whole set of drummers and all the young women who had been boarding with her. Many of the women who had been chanting ballads and lyrics now accompanied Aderonke's party, but she was the main attraction as the celebration moved down the street. Two of the ladies fanned her, and another carried an umbrella over her head.

When Aderonke arrived, she changed into her first set of special wedding clothes and then went around greeting people. People admired her dress and prayed that God would give her many children. She changed clothes several times. Each time she greeted her admirers, who offered prayers for her. Finally, she sat in a special chair, and everyone came by and placed money on her forehead. Someone sat nearby, discreetly recording the names and amounts—both so Aderonke could express her thanks and so that when gave her money, she would know how much to give the unmarried ones at their own weddings.

Just before sunset, Aderonke finally changed into the beautiful dress her mother had woven for her. She paraded around, then danced for everyone.

All the ladies began to dance with her as she bade farewell to her maidenhood.

Now Aderonke began her triumphal progress through the village. Her big moment was here, and she prayed that she would not be foolish and forget something important!

Beginning with the houses near the market square, Aderonke went from house to house. The drummers stayed outside with anyone who wanted to dance, and Aderonke went in to chant the part of her marriage lyric that referred to the family history of the people who lived there. If she did not know enough about that particular family's history, she'd sing some other part of the lyric that she had invented herself. If the people she was singing to were older than she was, she did the singing on her knees, and the lady of the house would lift her up when the song was over. Aderonke did not have to sing very long at each house; everyone realized how many houses she had to go to, so they lifted her to her feet after only a short time.

Aderonke did not have to get to every compound or every individual house, but she reached as many as she could before dark, ending at her own home. She knelt before her parents and chanted the history and praises of her own family, of people both alive and dead, of people who lived too far away to come to the wedding, and finally of her deceased grandparents. Eli broke down and wept loudly, embracing her daughter as she raised her to her feet and sang to her:

You will have many childrens;
You will have both boys and girls!
You will bring great honor to your husbands;
Your husband will be pleased with you!
Your husband will have a long life;
Your husband will cherish you all his life!
You will never have a rival;
The wicked will not harm you!
You will be blessed for the rest of your life;
You will be blessed in husband and children!
You will bring much joy to others;
Your husband will cherish you all his life!

Aderonke and her mother had a long talk that night while they packed Aderonke's belongings to take to her new home. Both women shed some tears—and neither one of them slept that night.

Long before dawn, five women from Remi's compound came to accompany Aderonke to her new home.

In another new dress, Aderonke knelt for the last time before her father and chanted part of her marriage lyric. Then he gave her his blessing in a song:

Your husband's life will last long;
Your own life will last long.
You will be blessed with children;
You will not suffer their deaths.
You will be blessed with many children;
You will be blessed with both boys and girls.
You will be blessed with cattle;
You will be blessed on your farm.
You will be blessed with rain and sun;
You will be blessed with a strong roof.
You will be honored in your family;
You will be honored in your village;
You will be honored by your husband;
You will be honored in your children!
Go now, my daughter!
Go to meet your husband!

At last, Aderonke was Remi's wife.

The drummers, all the girls who had been staying with Aderonk,e and a whole crowd of relatives turned out to take the bride to her husband. Her parents stayed behind; Aderonke was no longer part of their household.

The drummer started to drum. The girls and women started to sing. Aderonke put her shawl over her head and covered her face as well, and she put her father's straw hat on top of the shawl.

The entourage slowly wound its way from compound to compound, the women singing of Aderonke and her ancestors and the people coming out to greet them as they passed. When they came to the entrance of Remi's compound, the song changed, and all the chanting was now done by Remi's people.

Remi's father's sister washed Aderonke's feet with clear water and touched her chest with a kola nut, calling on her own father, who had been dead for many years, to protect the bride:

Jide, this is the wife of Remi!
Protect her from hardship;
Protect her from heartache;
Protect her from illness;
Protect her from injury.
Let her have many, many children.
Let her conceive children in her womb;
Let her carry them on her back!
Bless her with long life!
Let her and her husband, Remi,
Live long and enjoy each other!
Bless this beginning,
And bless them forevermore.

Then she touched Aderonke's chest with a white hen and said, "Aderonke, your head will fend for you! Your inner head will protect your outer head!"

The jubilant procession wound its way into the compound, singing and drumming. Aderonke chanted a lyric at the tomb of Remi's great-grandparents and at the shrine of the family god.

She went around the house and chanted a lyric to everyone there. Exhausted and almost out of voice, Aderonke finally settled in Tohun's room, which had been prepared for her. Tohun presented Aderonke with the bedclothes she had woven for her, and other clothes, including a shawl that Aderonke would have to use to cover her head for the next fourteen days. Aderonke dressed in these clothes. Keeping only the special dress, which would be saved for her own daughter's wedding, she gave the others she had worn, even her father's hat, as gifts to the women who had accompanied her. Aderonke would spend the next two weeks in this room, as was the village tradition.

According to the custom of their people, Remi was not supposed to be home when his wife arrived, so he was nowhere to be seen.

This was the beginning of 14 days of feasting and merriment, with drummers, dancers, acrobats, and clowns entertaining the guests. But the soon-to-be bride and groom were kept mostly apart, according to custom, only permitted brief visits and never alone until after the entire two-week wedding was complete.

Finally, they could be alone in each other's arms, and their love was so strong that on that day, they stayed in their room the whole day and never saw the sun—only each other's eyes.

**THE END**

# ABOUT THE AUTHOR

Felix Oguntoye, born and raised in Nigeria, is the grandchild of two different Nigerian traditional healers and medicine men who could call to the spirits of lost souls across great distances and harsh conditions, much as Aderonke's grandfather does in this debut novel. Raised in a westernized household but in a traditional village, he became fascinated by the storytellers of his village, and developed an interest in the Yoruba culture and rituals of his ancestors and neighbors. As a very young boy, he often assisted his grandmother selling smoked fish at the village market, where he got to know a very smart and talkative parrot—who liked to sing Yoruba folksongs along with the children.

Emigrating to the United States in 1974, Felix maintained frequent contact with Africa through a career in international trade that had him traveling around the world. He lives in the Atlanta area and has three grown children.

To contact Felix Oguntoye, please visit
parrotmatchmaker.com

This is the first of several books Felix intends to write. To be notified about future releases, please visit TheParrotMatchmaker.com/newbooks or turn the page over and send in the order/inquiry form.

# ORDER FORM

We are so glad you enjoyed THE PARROT MATCHMAKER. If you would like to order additional copies, please fill out and mail the form below.

| Quantity | Item | Price | Total |
|---|---|---|---|
| | *The Parrot Matchmaker* | $15.00 | |
| | Sales tax (7%) | | |
| | Shipping & Handling ($5.00) | | |
| | Subtotal | | |
| | TOTAL ORDER | | |

Ship to: _____

Address: _____

City: _____ State/Province: _____

Zip/Postal Code: _____ Country: _____

Phone: _____ Email : _____

Mail orders to:　Asalako Press
　　　　　　　　　P.O.Box 487
　　　　　　　　　Pine Lake, GA 30072

Inquiries: admin@asalakopress.com

Check us out on the web: http://www.ParrotMatchmaker.com

www.ingramcontent.com/pod-product-compliance
Lightning Source LLC
Chambersburg PA
CBHW070833250626
47159CB00003B/760